A SUMMER IN HARLEM

Brendan Whitt Copyright © 2013 Brendan Whitt

ISBN: 0615883400

ISBN-13: 978-0615883403

DEDICATION

This book is dedicated to the late Dr. Paul Skalski and my grandmother Opal Beatrice Whitt.

ACKNOWLEDGMENTS

I would like to thank my family and my girlfriend for being my top supporters, my good friend and mentor Kevin Ray, my cover artist Dakarai Ashby reppin Lame Brotherhood, and most of all you. Without you there would be no need for my writing. Thank you.

Peace....

Chapter 1

"Thad, Thad, Thaddeus Leon Thomas! If I gotta call your name one more time to get up boy!" The loud and bellowing voice forced Thad to wake up. He pulled his blanket from over his head as the sun shined brightly through his bedroom window and into his face. He sat up for a moment and rubbed the sleep from his eyes before letting out a big yawn. Standing in the doorway staring at him was his grandmother. She was a large and portly black woman with a head full of grey hair. Standing right behind her was her fat yellowish orange cat named Precious.

"Glad to see you're finally up," his grandmother said. "I'm headed out to run a few errands. Your breakfast is downstairs but you have to make your own eggs. You know how they get when their cold. When I get back we can head for the train station." She took two steps out of Thad's room before turning around, "Oh, and feed Precious" she added. Almost instinctively Precious turned around and followed Thad's grandmother out of the room. When he could hear her footsteps heading down the stairs he pulled his covers completely off of his body and got out of bed. Thad was a relatively scrawny kid with dark skin and short black hair. He had just finished his first year of high school and had aspirations of becoming an engineer after college. He wanted to go to Tuskegee where one of his idols George Washington Carver had taught. Thad was a very intelligent kid who always garnered high praise from his teachers in regards to his academic accomplishments and behavior. He rarely got into any serious trouble or mischief. Outside of school Thad hung out with his same friends from when he was a child. He was just your run of the mill teenager from Beloit, Alabama in 1948.

Thad stumbled out of bed and headed towards the bathroom. He brushed his teeth then washed his face with a hot rag. When he was finished Thad walked back into his room and sat on his bed. "She never makes my eggs," he mumbled to himself. "She can kiss my ass, I'm not makin' my own eggs." On the chair in his room was a collared shirt with a pair of trousers. He put them on and made his way downstairs. Since his Grandmother was gone he decided to turn on the radio and listen to his favorite genre of music, Jazz. Thad especially loved swing music. The liveliness of the instruments always made him think of life outside of Beloit. Thad loved Jazz but his Grandmother hated it. She called it "that bullshit music". Thad's grandmother was a god fearing woman who's preference were gospel hymns. Thad loved Jazz because of how every musician could play their own part of the song the way they wanted to but still manage to sound like one cohesive collective of musicians. He sat down with his bowl of grits and the few strips of bacon his grandmother had left him while he listened to the radio.

When he finished eating, Thad went back upstairs to grab his luggage. Thad's grandmother told him that she would send him to Harlem to visit his Aunt Bird and three cousins for a few weeks over the summer if he was able keep his grades up. Thad did more than that, he finished his freshman year at the top of his class. "Finally," he thought to himself "a nice long trip to Harlem. I get to ride in a cab, see the city, and most of all listen to live Jazz music." Thad was more than excited to be headed to New York City. This was the trip of a lifetime. No one he knew from Beloit got to go to the Big Apple for three weeks.

When Thad's Grandmother got back from running her errands she yelled up the stairs for him. "Thad, you ready to go?" she asked.

"Here I come Grandma," he yelled back down. Thad grabbed his bags and headed down stairs. His grandmother handed him twenty-five dollars and a small brown bag filled with snacks. "Now this money should last you while you're up there and this is a small snack for your train ride. It should hold you over until your stop in Chicago."

"Thank you. Do you want me to call when I get to New York?"

"Yes. And be sure to look out for your Aunt Bird. You remember what she looks like?" Thad had no idea what his Aunt Bird looked like. He had only seen her twice his entire life and he was only about three years old the last time he had even seen her. All of the photos in the house of her and Thad's mother were from the twenties before Thad and his cousins had even been born.

"Not really." he said.

"Well you know she's tall and scrawny with itty bitty chicken legs. Just look for a lady who looks somethin' like your mother."

"Oh yeah I know what she looks like now." Thad was lying right through his teeth. He still had no clue of what Aunt Bird looked like. In fact, Thad had never even seen his mother. His widowed Grandmother had taken him in when he was born after Thad's mother had died from complications during childbirth. He kept a picture of her on his nightstand to remind him of her. The only thing on his mind at the moment was getting out of Beloit and enjoying the beginning of his summer in Harlem. "I'll be sure to keep an eye out." he said.

Outside waiting for Thad and his grandmother was Mr. Harris who stayed down the road on his old family farm that didn't grow much of anything. He was a tall fat man with very dark skin. His English was so bad that when combined with his southern accent the words came out sounding like gibberish. Mr. Harris had an old red pickup truck that was covered in rust. He had agreed to take Thad and his Grandmother to the train station. Thad hated catching rides from Mr. Harris during the school year. The inside of his pickup was full of trash and old cigarette butts. "Grandma you couldn't find nobody else with a car," Thad desperately asked.

"Boy you be thankful," his grandmother snapped. "It's only a thirty-five minute drive. You will not die from riding in his truck. And make sure you say thank you." Thad walked outside carrying his bags and set them in the bed of the truck.

"Thanks for the ride Mr. Harris." he said.

"Buah you know I can geh you a ride wheneva you need." Mr. Harris said. Thad got into the truck and slid to the middle of the seat leaving enough room for his grandmother on the end. The smell of old cigarette butts was enough to make a person cover their mouth and nose. Mr. Harris leaned over and whispered to Thad, "No smoking whyle da lady in da cah now. Mannas." Thad just stared at Mr. Harris before turning to the window, "Grandma we ready" he shouted.

As they drove down the road towards the train station Mr. Harris couldn't help but to yap away. It was probably his favorite thing to do behind smoking. "Buah I tell ya, New Yawk is a big ol' place. I had seent it way back ya hear. Buildins that go so high up you cain't even see da tops of em ya hear. I mean, big ol buildins. Its way bigguh dan down here in Beloit ya hear." Thad was tired of listening to Mr. Harris' jibberish. He knew Mr. Harris was lying anyway. The only sound Thad wanted to hear was a loud train's horn rumbling down the track followed by an "All aboard!" from the train conductor. At least by then he would know that he was that much closer to Harlem.

After a nerly forty minute drive down a long dusty road and hearing Mr. Harris' gibberish, Thad could see the train station off in the distance. Thad couldn't believe it. He was finally headed to New York City. He checked to make sure his ticket was in his pocket. He pulled it out and scanned it over before shoving it back into his pocket. Thad's grandmother got out of the truck followed by Thad. Mr. Harris got out to help Thad unload his bags from the truck bed. That was the only thing he wanted Mr. Harris to do. "You enjoy yaself ya hear." Mr. Harris said.

"I will" Thad responded smiling. Thad and his grandmother walked to the entrance of the train station.

"Want me to wait with you," his grandmother asked.

"Nah, I'm fine." he said.

"Ok then. Well remember to be safe and don't get into any trouble. And hold on to that money. Don't fall for no hustles. You don't know what people can be like in that city."

"Yes ma'am." he said. "And I'll be sure to give you a call when I get there."

"Ok. Love you and be safe". She gave Thad a big hug accompanied with a kiss on the cheek. As she walked away Thad could feel freedom and excitement sweep across his body. He was so happy to get out of little old Beloit and go see the world. While waiting on a bench facing the tracks Thad saw a man in an old dirty brown hat drawing a crowd of onlookers. The man was middle aged and black with a light skin complexion. Thad was curious to see what the old man was doing to cause so much commotion. He decided to stay where he was and watch the spectacle from a distance. The man had a piece of cardboard on top of a garbage can with three playing card on top of the cardboard. "If you can find the Jack of spades I'll pay you two dollars, any Challengers? Just find the jack for two dollars." The crowd of onlookers just stood around looking and talking amongst each other when a little boy who looked no older than six walked up to the man and placed two dollars down. "Where'd you get so much money from little boy," the man asked. The boy didn't respond. He gave the man a blank stare as the crowd continued to watch.

"Which one is the jack lil' man?" The boy pointed to the card on the left. "You sure?" The boy nodded his head yes. The man took a moment to flip the card. As he flipped the card over the man had a look of disbelief on his face before quickly turning it into a smile. He handed the two dollar bills along with the two he had bet to the little boy. The boy took the four dollars and walked away. "Win some you lose some." he said. "Who's next?" Suddenly another middle aged man, this one white, walked up and placed two dollars down onto the old piece of cardboard. The old man shuffled the three cards and randomly placed them face down. The white man chose the card on the left. When the hustler flipped the card over it was the three of hearts. "Aww Goddammit!" the man shouted. Thad wanted to get closer but he didn't want to risk being called out. The little boy winning two bucks was tempting to Thad but the one thing his grandmother told him not to do was lose any money to any shady people, so he decided to stay put and continue to watch from his spot on the bench.

The next contestant to walk up was a heavy set black woman and her husband. "I know this trick you old drunk, I got four dollars." she said slamming the bills down onto the makeshift table. The hustler shuffled his cards and removed his hat to expose his balding head. "Then choose your card ma'am." he said politely.

"The middle card you sneaky bastard" she snapped. The hustler flipped the card revealing the eight of clubs. The old man simply smiled. "Guess you don't this game well enough." he said. The hustler packed up his things and walked away. As the crowd began to disperse, Thad stood up and looked down the tracks to see if the train was coming.

Thad was growing more and more anxious by the minute. He had pulled out his ticket to look at it about ten times to make sure it was still in his pocket. Since him being so impatient wasn't making time speed up, Thad decided to look in the brown bag his grandmother had packed for him. He had two sandwiches, one was a peanut butter and jelly sandwich while the other was a ham sandwich. He had one soda and the bottom of the bag was filled with a few of his grandmothers homemade cookies. He pulled out a cookie and began to nibble on it while he continued to wait on the train. Several minutes later Thad could hear a train engine barreling down the tracks. "Finally" he thought to himself. The moment he had been waiting for since the last day of school was here. He picked up his bags and held his ticket in his hand. When the train pulled up a huge plume of dark smoke escaped from the top of the train's smoke stack. Thad looked up and marveled at the size of the train. The cars stretched as far as he could see and had a shiny metal coat with a few thin red lines going down the sides.

The speakers over the platform crackled as a voice rang out, "P & R leaving for Chicago now boarding." Thad walked to the colored car and stood in line to board with the other blacks. While he was standing in line Thad noticed the hustler sneaking onto the back of the train. When he got to the front of the line he presented his ticket and proceeded to board. When he finally got on board Thad walked down the aisle until he found his seat. It was a small area with a window just large enough for Thad to look out and see all of the different changes in scenery during his trip. He sat down and put his bags in the seat across from him. "Ten hours until we stop in Chicago," he thought to himself. He decided to catch up on the sleep he had missed after being awakened by his grandmother earlier that morning. As the train began to pull off Thad slowly drifted off to sleep as he gently rocked along with the train as it barreled down the tracks. He knew he wouldn't be able to get off of the train in Chicago but seeing the city's skyline would be a good preview of New York.

A few hours later when he woke up, Thad looked out the window to see how far the train had gotten. All he could see were rolling green pastures and a farm house or barn every few miles or so. He knew they hadn't gotten too far from Beloit, the train could still be in Alabama for all he knew. It took Thad a while to realize the little boy sitting across from him. He had taken Thad's luggage and placed it next to him while he was sleeping. When Thad took a closer look at the boy's face he realized it was the kid from the platform who had won the two dollars from

15

the old man. Thad blankly stared at the boy who stared right back. After a few moments of awkward silence the little boy finally spoke up.

"Sorry I moved your stuff," he said. "I just wanted to sit down. My name's Fitz by the way. Lil' Fitz."

"I'm Thad. What you doin on a Train all alone anyway?"

"I'm not alone. My dad's here with me."

Thad was confused. "But back at the station you were by yourself."

"My dad was the man with the cards."

Thad looked surprised. "So you knew which card to pick," he asked.

"Yep. I always know. He tells me which one is the jack and I pick it. Then more people show up. Sometimes he loses but most of the time he wins."

"So you guys are hustlers?"

"That's what my dad calls it."

Thad looked up and happened to see one of the rail workers checking tickets. He looked at Fitz and looked back up. He knew Fitz didn't have a ticket but he also didn't want the kid to get into any trouble. Fitz got up and hid underneath Thad's seat. "Hey kid, what you doin'?" Fitz put his finger to his lips signaling Thad to be quiet. Thad sat straight up in his seat and watched the rail worker make his way towards him. "Ticket please." the rail worker asked. Thad pulled out his ticket and showed it to him. He kept his composures as best he could but on the inside he was a nervous wreck. If anyone saw Fitz hiding underneath his seat Thad risked the chance of being kicked off of the train. "Thank you." the rail worker said. He shot Thad a quick smile before heading into the next car. Fitz reemerged from under Thad's seat and sat back down.

"You can't just do that," Thad said. "I coulda' just got kicked off."

"It's ok. I do it all the time." Fitz said.

"What if you woulda' got caught, then what?"

"I just tell them I snuck on with my dad." he said. "One time the people on the train felt so bad they let us ride all the way to the next city. My dad told me don't get caught so I just started doing that."

"You're a smart kid. Where'd you get the name Lil Fitz?"

"My dad's name is Fitzgerald Wallace, so my mom named me Fitzgerald Wallace Jr. But everybody just calls me Lil' Fitz."

"Where's your mom?"

"In Baltimore. That's where I'm From. He picked me up from school one day and we hopped on a bus and left. We been riding the trains ever since."

"Miss your mom at all?"

"Yeah but my dad says I'll see her soon." Thad was growing skeptical of Fitz's story. "What kind of dad takes his son away from his mom and hops trains," he thought to himself. He knew there was something else to the story. He just couldn't figure out what.

"What does your dad do with all of the money he wins?"

"Buys us food and get us hotel rooms."

"He doesn't have a house or somethin' in Baltimore?"

"No. He used to live with me and my mom until they got into a fight. I didn't see him for a while until the day he came and got me from school."

"So let me get this right," Thad started "he wins all

that money and you guys don't live in a house somewhere? Where are you guys headed?"

"I don't know. Back home I guess." Fitz looked out the window, "Sometimes he spends his money on this brown stuff," he said.

"What is it," Thad asked.

"I don't know. He has this needle and he heats up the brown stuff. Then he puts it in his arm. It might be medicine but the one time I saw him using it he got really mad. So now he only does it when I'm sleep." Thad had no idea what Fitz was talking about. At that moment Fitz's dad came walking down the aisle. He walked over to the seats Thad and Fitz were sitting in. He had a soda in his hand that he handed to Fitz.

"Hey lil' man, who's your friend", he asked.

"His name is Thad."

"Nice to meet you Thad", He shook Thad's hand before continuing his conversation with his son. "We're gettin off in Chicago. I got the people to let us stay on until then. I got us a few empty seats." Fitz smiled and stood up, "See Thad", he said while smiling "it always works out." Fitz and his dad got up and headed to another car. Thad wished the best for his young friend Fitzgerald Wallace Jr. As the train made it's way closer to Chicago Thad could feel himself getting sleepy again. Thad figured if he caught a quick nap he could wake up in time to see Chicago before the train refueled and headed off to it's final destination in New York.

When he woke up it was completely dark outside. Thad saw no bright lights, no people walking around outside, or even a train station. It was pitch black. It took Thad a while to realize the train wasn't headed to Chicago, the train had already passed it. The train had refueled while Thad was fast asleep and was already headed for New York. Thad was upset about missing Chicago. He wasn't sure when he would get the chance to see Chicago again. At the same time he grew more anxious to see New York. Since it was late Thad decided to eat the ham sandwich his grandmother had packed for him before going back to sleep. As he drifted off , Thad hoped the next time he opened his eyes he would be looking at the New York skyline.

Chapter 2

The next morning Thad woke up with the sun shining brightly in his face through the window. Outside all he could see were cornfields. He figured the train wasn't anywhere close to New York. By now Thad had finished all of the food his grandmother had packed for him. He was beginning to get a little hungry but decided to wait until he got to his Aunt's house. Thad stepped out into the aisle to stretch for a bit since he had been sitting the entire ride. Ahead of him was an older married couple. He decided to go over and ask them if they knew where the train was.

"Excuse me," Thad politely interjected "how far are we from New York?"

"We just entered Pennsylvania. You headed to New York too?" the husband asked.

"Yeah, I'm goin' to visit some family in Harlem."

"I haven't been to Harlem in years. They say it ain't the same."

"How so?" Thad became a bit curious.

"Well it ain't how it used to be. The clubs not as

packed, the music scene ain't the same, and it's full of old musicians lookin for a fix. Harlem done changed from what I heard." The husband quickly switched the subject. "So where you from, don't sound like you from up here" he said.

"I'm not, I'm from Alabama." Thad answered

"No kiddin'. What part?"

"Beloit."

"Hmm, never heard of it."

"You know how much longer we have until we're in New York?" Thad said.

"I'd say about three of four more hours."

"Thank you," Thad said. The man and his wife both gave Thad a smile. As he made his way back to his seat he sat down and continued to look out of the window. There wasn't much to keep him occupied for the rest of the trip seeing as how his excitement had long since subsided. Now he was just waiting to see a skyline since he had missed Chicago's. He decided to look at his mother's picture to try and get a good idea of what Aunt bird looked like. It was the only thing he could do to take his mind off of the rest of his boring train ride. Outside was beginning to look too much like home so he shifted his attention elsewhere.

After doing one time consuming task after another Thad was becoming restless. He couldn't sit still, he was hungry, and taking a nap was impossible since all he did was sleep for most of the train ride. Just as his patience was beginning to wear thin Thad could see something in the distance. He sat up and focused on whatever it was. After a while he started to make out the figures in the distance. They were skyscrapers. Thad couldn't believe it. He was finally getting closer to New York. Just then the loudspeakers on the train crackled. Thad was anticipating good news. He quickly perked up in his seat and gave the speaker his full attention as if his teacher had just walked into the classroom. "Attention all passengers, we will be pulling into the station shortly. Please make sure you have removed all of your luggage and belongings before departing from the train. Thank you."

After the loud speaker crackled again before turning off Thad quickly grabbed his bags and sat in the seat closest to the aisle. Alabama was the furthest thing from his mind at the moment Thad was in the Big Apple. As he admired it's beauty from a distance, The Empire State Building overlooked every other building in the city . "Mr. Harris was right," he thought to himself "these buildings sure is tall." When the train turned into the station Thad looked out of the window from an empty seat. He had never seen so many people in one place in his entire life. The station had to be full of Beloit's entire population. When the train finally came to a complete stop he grabbed his bags and departed as quickly as his legs could carry him. He was so wrapped up in the moment that he had completely forgotten to look for Aunt Bird. He found a bench where he could sit and look out for her although he still wasn't sure of what she looked like.

After what seemed like the longest five minute wait of his life, Thad felt a tap on his shoulder. When he turned around it was a tall older woman. "Wow, you sure have grown up," she said. It was Aunt Bird, his mother's older sister. "Come give me a hug, don't be shy." Thad was shocked at how much she resembled his mother in the picture. She was a tall skinny woman with long legs. Her voice sounded how he always imagined his mother's voice to sound. Very calm, light, and soothing. She smelled like the prettiest perfume he had ever smelled and her skin was a nice caramel complexion. She was beautiful

She reached for one of Thad's bags, "Let me help you with those sweetheart." Thad handed her the lighter bag and the two walked out of the station and onto the busy street. Thad's eyes grew big as he saw all of the cars and buildings and people in fancy clothes. This was the New York he had always imagined. He didn't care about what the guy on the train was talking about. Thad knew the city would be as beautiful as he dreamt it would be. Every billboard ad looked as if it had been ripped from one of his grandmother's catalogs and blown up for everyone to see. When he looked back down at the street it was full of taxis and other cars. He quickly pulled out his money, "I have cab fare," he said.

"That's ok sweetheart, I got it" she said while chuckling. When Aunt Bird finally flagged down a cab they grabbed Thad's things and got in. Thad didn't take his eyes off of the scenery for one second. He wanted to soak up as much of the city as he could. In the country every family had maybe one car for the entire family if they could afford it. Some families had no car so the roads were rarely ever full. You could race with your buddies Saturday night and never have to worry about getting into an accident. In New York the entire street was filled with cars and buses and trucks. And it wasn't just one street. On every street it seemed like there was traffic from one intersection to the next. Thad hoped the scenery in Harlem was as beautiful as this.

The further the cab drove the less busy the streets were. The billboards were now far and few in between. He was expecting to see big beautiful jazz clubs and people in fancy clothes getting out of really expensive cars. Instead Harlem was turning out to be the polar opposite. Many of the streets were beginning to be full of abandoned and decayed buildings. Thad wasn't sure what to make of it all. When the cab finally stopped in front of a medium sized apartment building Aunt Bird paid the driver and grabbed the bag she was carrying. "We're here" she said. Thad grabbed his other bag and got out of the cab. As the cab sped off Thad took a look at his surroundings. Across the street a little further down from where he was standing was an old night club called "The Noble Veronica". The windows were boarded up and the doors were chained. The kids in the front of the building were playing with pieces of the wood that had broken off of one of the windows. Now he knew what the man on the train was talking about. Harlem was a completely different Harlem from what Thad heard and read about. He remembered hearing of the great authors, poets, artists, and musicians who had flourished there just a few decades prior. The only thing Thad didn't hear about was the state of decay Harlem was now facing.

"The elevator's out so we have to walk up to our floor" Aunt Bird said. "We only live on the eighth floor." Thad looked at Aunt Bird as if she was crazy. Carrying luggage up eight flights of stairs sounded horrible. The two started up the stairs as she asked Thad all types of questions to further break the ice and get to know her nephew a little better.

"So how old are you now" she asked.

"I'll be fifteen right before school starts. How old is Willie? Grandma said he's close to my age."

"He's seventeen, he'll be eighteen in October. You

know I have two little girls too don't you?"

"Yeah. Daisy and Denise right?"

"Yep, eight and five. My three little babies."

"Willie isn't a baby, he's almost grown" Thad joked, making Aunt Bird laugh.

"When you're a mother they'll always be your babies" she said. When they finally got to the eighth floor they both let out a huge sigh of relief. They walked a few doors down before reaching #805. Aunt Bird opened the door and walked in with Thad right behind her. The apartment was bigger than what he expected. There was a radio in the corner with a clock on the wall. Surrounding the clock was a bunch of pictures. "Here I'll take those." Aunt Bird said. "You'll be staying in Willies room. He offered." Thad looked back to the wall and saw a picture of his mother just like the one he always carried. Next to the radio was a big navy blue leather chair and next to it was a long couch the same style and color. Across from that was a love seat that matched. The table in the middle of the floor was covered in magazines.

Aunt Bird came back out with two little girls right behind her. Girls come meet your cousin Thad. First there was Daisy who was the youngest. She had a missing front tooth with pig tails and one bow on each one. Denise was a bit older and took directly after Aunt Bird. She was tall for her age and thin.

"Hi Thad." Daisy said. "Nice to meet you."

"He dress like he goin' to school." Denise joked.

"He's dressed like a young presentable man," Aunt Bird said "like a gentleman." Thad acknowledged her compliment with a grin.

"I wanna know what the south is like." Daisy said.

"Well," Thad started "it's hot pretty much most of the year, it can get pretty cold sometimes. It's not as busy as it is here and the air smells better."

"Air ain't got no smell." Denise snapped.

"Well when you get older and visit down south you'll see what I'm talkin' about."

"How's school going for you?" Aunt Bird asked.

"It's goin' good." Thad replied. "I'll be a sophomore this fall. Hopefully when I graduate I can go to Tuskegee to study engineering."

"What's that?" asked Denise.

"Engineers are the people who take ideas and build

stuff from those ideas." Thad replied.

Daisy's face turned up in disdain, "Sounds boring." she said. "Me and Denise gon sing Jazz and be in a group called the 'Shine Brights.'"

"I told you I don't like that name." Denise said.

"Well I don't see you comin' up with nothin' better."

"Cause I'm thinkin' of one better than the Shine Brights."

"Well Willie should be back any minute" Aunt Bird said. "C'mon girls, We gotta finish dinner."

Aunt Bird and the girls made their way to the kitchen. Thad decided to sit down and relax for a minute. He wondered how long until Willie would be home. The thing that excited him the most about his visit was meeting Willie. Thad got up and walked over to the window. Outside he could see a handful of cars driving down the street and a random bus. There were plenty of people walking around outside. More than what Thad was used to seeing back home. There were laundry lines that hung from people's windows. Thad had never seen an area this busy. He had visited Mobile a few times but it was nothing like this.

When Thad sat back down he turned on the radio.
The stations were different from the stations he listened to
back home. After trying to find something to listen to he
turned off the radio and sat in silence. As Thad continued
to sit in the chair someone opened the door as a voice
rang out, "Momma I'm back!" The voice sounded as if it
was a boy close to Thad's age. He turned around and saw
Willie standing in the doorway. He had on gym shorts, a
pair of sneakers, and a basketball in his hand. Willie was
a little taller than Thad and was a little lighter too. Willie
looked at Thad, "Thad? My country cousin? Whats up
man?"

"Hey." Thad replied.

"Give me a sec, we'll chat." Willie walked to the
back of the apartment and reemerged a few moments
later. "So What's up?" he said. Willie was the type of
person who could sit down and hold an entire
conversation with you like you two were the best of
friends, and it would be the first time you ever met the
guy.

"I'm just amazed at this city." Thad said. "I assume
there's plenty to do around here."

"Not when you lived here all your life. Same ol' shit everyday to me. especially here in Harlem. How's Alabama? Hot and full of fresh air I suppose."

"Pretty much." Thad replied.

"Chasin' them country girls around too ain't you?"

Thad blushed. He never had a girlfriend or even kissed a girl. "Not really." he said, "I just focus on school for right now.

"Real bookworm type." replied Willie. "I can respect it. Everybody likes a smart kid. You see the room yet?" Willie asked. Thad shook his head no.

"C'mon." Willie said as he led Thad down the hall. The hallway was the only area that lead you through the rest of the apartment. It was so narrow that you could reach your arms out and touch both walls. They were covered in a pink striped wallpaper. There were three doors in the hallway. The only door on the left was Willie's room. Willie opened the door and set Thad's bags next to a chair in the corner.

"You can sleep in here. Ima sleep on the couch while you visit." Willie said. "You can see a little bit from the window. People like to play on that corner." Willie pulled

back the shade to show Thad what he was talking about.
Across the street Thad could see one corner of the Noble
Veronica across the street and a little bit of the sidewalk
in front of it which was cracked and dingy. "They usually
only out at night." Willie said. Thad was hoping the
'playing' that Willie was talking about referred to the
playing of instruments, specifically jazz instruments.
"Then over here is my closet." Willie said. "I cleared out
a little bit of space for you." Thad set his bags in the
closet and walked back over to the bed.

"You like to read at all?" asked Thad.

"If it ain't for school hell no. Why you ask?"

"Just wanted to know if you had any books I could
read. I'll just listen to the radio out there."

"I had one in here but my sisters broke it playin'
around." Willie led Thad back out into the front living
room. "Only thing left to do now is go out and see the
neighborhood if you want."

"Sure." Thad said.

"Ma! Me and Thad goin' out front. We'll be back."
Willie shouted. Aunt Bird's voice carried lightly through
the hall but it was still loud enough to hear. "Ok." she

said. Willie grabbed a key off of the table in the living room. He led Thad to the steps and they walked down to the first floor. When The two boys got outside they both looked around. There were a few people walking around and the same kids playing in front of The Noble Veronica from earlier. "Ain't too much goin' on out here on the frontline" Willie said. "Guess we'll walk down to the corner and back." Willie was talking to Thad but Thad was more focused on how many buildings were on the street. Each one had people either sitting or standing in front of it. There was a car passing every second it seemed. The city had him mesmerized. When they got to the corner Thad heard Willie's voice cut back in, "This pretty much all of it this way." he said. Thad had missed the entire conversation. He was strangely drawn to the allure of Harlem. It wasn't the Harlem he expected but it was still Harlem nonetheless.

On the way back to the apartment Thad saw a couple of guys shooting dice on the side of a building. "Ay Willie," one of them yelled out "what's happenin' man?"

"Nothin' much." Willie replied. He and Thad continued to walk past them. "That's Dino and a couple of his boys." Willie said. "All they do is get into trouble. Shoot dice and do stick ups. That's it." He turned to Thad, "Ever shoot craps?" he asked.

"No," Thad replied " but I can play poker".

"Never played it." Willie said.

When they got back upstairs Willie went back into the apartment with Thad following behind him. "I gotta wash up." he said. "Food should be done in a minute." Thad wanted to wash up too but he saw Willie needed it more. After all Willie had just gotten back home from playing basketball. That didn't take the feeling away of sitting in the same clothes for an entire day on a train. He walked back into Willie's room to grab what he wanted to put on after his bath. Thad walked into the closet and pulled out one of his bags. Since it was the beginning of June the temperature was a little warm. Thad decided to open the window to get some fresher and hopefully cooler air. When he opened the window Thad could see a man on the corner with a saxophone looking as if he was getting ready to play it. He blew a test note before beginning to play. Thad sat on the edge of the bed as he listened.

Although his grandmother hated Jazz Thad still found a way to listen to "that bullshit music". Thad never paid her any attention when it came to music. He loved Jazz and felt it was the greatest form of American music ever to be created. This was the first time however he had heard live Jazz music. He closed his eyes and continued to listen as the man continued to play. Thad began to vision himself as the saxophone player on the corner. He imagined he was inside of the Noble Veronica which had a full house tonight. He imagined what the inside might look like and how he'd have his bandstand set up. A few trumpet players, a drummer, and one of those white boys who could play a guitar. "I would have the baddest band in all of the land." Thad thought to himself.

In the middle of his dream he saw a beautiful girl in the front row. She was at a table all alone staring directly at him. He saw her mouth move as if she was whispering something to him. He looked at her as she mouthed his name. Now she had his full attention. The next time she said his name he heard her. "Thad," she said seductively. "Thad." When he opened his eyes Willie was standing in the doorway. "Hey Thad," he said "my mom's almost done cookin'. You can come sit down if you want."

"Alright." he said. Thad got up and went out into the hallway. Eating his first home cooked meal since leaving was more important than a quick bath. When he came out of Willie's room he saw two doors on the other side of the hall. The first was directly across the hall. The door was open and revealed a small but neatly kept bathroom. There was a bath tub with a toilet next to it. Behind the door was a sink and mirror. A few steps down was another door. It was closed so he assumed it was where Aunt Bird slept. Since there was no other room he assumed the girls slept in the bed with their mother. As Thad walked into the kitchen he saw the girls setting up the table while Aunt Bird was standing at the stove. "Did you call Grandma?" she asked.

"Not yet." Thad replied.

"You should call and tell her you made it. The phone is in there on the table behind the couch."

"I'll go call her now." he said. He walked into the living room and looked behind the couch. He saw the phone sitting exactly where Aunt Bird said it would be. He picked it up and called his Grandmother. The phone rang a few times before Thad heard his grandmother pick it up.

"Hello." she answered.

"Hey Grandma. I'm at Aunt Bird's."

"Good. When'd you get in?"

"About a few hours ago."

"Alright," she said "you enjoy yourself and I'll talk to you later baby."

"Alright Grandma. Love you."

"Love you too." she said before hanging up the phone.

When Thad walked back into the kitchen everyone was at the table except for Aunt Bird who was pulling corn muffins out of the oven. The kitchen table was over by the wall on the left side of the kitchen. Everyone had a side of their own at the rectangular table. Willie sat at one end with Daisy and Denise sitting on the two sides closest to him. The seat at the other end was empty. Next to Daisy whose back was turned to the stove and refrigerator on the right side of the kitchen was an empty chair. Thad decided to sit down and wait for everyone to start grabbing their food first. When Aunt Bird sat the muffins on the table everyone began to help themselves.

"So you two getting along pretty well?" Aunt Bird asked.

"Yeah. We gettin' to know each other and what not." Willie said.

"That's good." Aunt Bird turned her attention to Thad. "How's the food Thad?" she asked.

"It's amazing" he said with a mouth full. Aunt Bird had made a full spread that day. She had fried up some crispy chicken and made some home made mashed potatoes. She took a little of the chicken grease and made her own brown gravy. To go along with that was a side of corn and golden corn muffins.

"It tastes just as good as Grandma's."

"That's who taught me." she said. After dinner everyone placed their dishes in the sink. The girls helped Aunt Bird clean as Willie and Thad went back into the living room. Willie turned on the radio and tuned it to a station playing some music as they sat and listened.

"I saw you lookin' at Catfish out there." Willie said.

"Who?"

"The dude you was lookin' at earlier playin' the sax.

That was Catfish. He used to get booked around here a lot when I was a kid. He all messed up now."

"He sounded good to me."

"I wasn't talkin' about his music. But yeah he can still play." Willie said. "You wanna go see some cats play later on tonight?" he asked.

"Cats play what?"

"Music."

"Watch Cats play music?"

Willie let out a loud bellowing laugh. "Not like kitty cats. Dudes like us. Kids our age playin' music. Just like what you hear on the radio. You know Charlie Parker and Bob Crosby, guys like them?"

"Ohhhh yeahhhh. But why'd you call 'em cats?"

"Because they're cool cats. It's just the way we talk up here. You can take that back to Alabama with you when you leave." Willie joked.

Aunt Bird was standing in the hall. "Willie can you come here for a moment?" she said. Willie got up and followed her to his room. She closed the door and sat down in the chair in the corner. "Now you know what I wanna talk about don't you" she asked. Willie just shrugged his shoulders. "Well since you don't remember I'll tell you this, If you have my sister's son out there in those streets gettin' into trouble I'm gon' let them take you away this time. Got it?" The look on her face stuck until Willie agreed with what she just said. "He's all I got left of her and I want you to treat him like a brother and look out for him." She got up and walked over to the door. "Now remember what I said." After she said her piece she walked across the hall and went into her room to get ready for work.

Willie went back into the living room. "Now where were we?" he said while walking back to where he was sitting before his mother had called for him. "Oh yeah. You listen to Jazz at all back home?"

"Sometimes but Grandma don't like it too much. She says its shit. You'd be bored down there. Nothin' like this at all."

"Man you don't know how many times my mom asked me if I wanted to visit. I don't wanna go down there and look at Grandma all day. Lemme guess," Willie started "she loves listenin' to hymns and gospel and shit like that?" Thad laughed and shook his head yes. "And

41

that's why I told my mom I don't wanna go."

"It's all she listens to." Thad said. "All day until she goes to sleep. She bought me a radio to listen to music on but she doesn't let me listen to jazz."

"A real shame" Willie said.

Later that evening Aunt Bird was getting ready to head out for work. The girls were already in bed. Willie was waiting to sneak out a few hours after his mother had left for work. "Yo Thad," he said "I got a move for us. There's this place a few blocks away me and my boys go to from time to time. I'm wearin' a suit, you can dress how you want. Just dress to impress."

Thad remembered he hadn't gotten the chance to take a bath. He wasn't too big on dress clothes and had already made up in his mind what he wanted to wear. When him and Willie were done talking Thad went into the room and grabbed his clothes. There was a knock at the door, it was Aunt Bird. She cracked the door and poked her head through, "I'm headed off to work, Ill see you in the morning." she said.

"Ok." Thad replied.

She closed the door as Thad looked for what he was

going to wear since he didn't like to wear suits. He grabbed a nice sweatshirt and a pair of slacks. Thad went into the bathroom and got in the tub. When he was done getting dressed Thad went out into the living room and sat down. Willie was on the phone. When he hung up Willie turned to Thad.

"That's what you decided to wear?" he said.

"What? I hate wearing suits."

"If you say so." Willie walked around to the other side of the couch. When he looked down he saw Thad was wearing a pair of sneakers. "You wearin canvas All-Stars too? Man you done took the cake." Willie started to laugh.

Although Aunt Bird wasn't home Willie still had to sneak out of the apartment. There were too many neighbors that would tell her if they saw Willie sneaking out at night. "Alright," he said "you go stand in the kitchen and wait for me." Thad walked to the kitchen and waited for Willie. Willie turned both locks on the front door and left the lamp in the living room on. Then he went in and turned off the bathroom light before turning off his bedroom light. He opened the door to check on his sisters who were still sleeping. After that he made his way to the kitchen before turning off the kitchen light. "We gotta go out onto the fire escape to get down onto the street." he said. Thad hadn't noticed it earlier but there was a door by the refrigerator that was painted the same color as the wall. In passing it was easy to walk into the kitchen and not realize a door was there. Willie unlocked and opened the door before slipping the key into his shoe. Thad walked out first as Willie followed behind him. He turned around to close and locked the door as Thad marveled at the beautifully lit night sky. The quiet busyness of New York at night was a sight and sound to behold.

Thad and Willie walked down the fire escape steps as quietly as they could before Willie led Thad down an alley way. "We can follow this alley out to the street the party is on. Don't want the cops takin' us in" Willie said. Thad didn't know they would have to dodge the cops on the way.

"What kind of place are we going to anyway?" Thad asked. "You said it was in the neighborhood."

"Just relax. It's a place a few block away. We'll be

there in no time." Willie said. Thad was growing weary about being out so late in the big city. He didn't want to worry about dodging random patrolmen all night but there wasn't much to do back in the apartment anyway. He decided going out for a night on the town wasn't going to be too bad. Willie didn't give him a reason not to feel safe. He seemed confident enough that his route to wherever they were headed was a safe one. Besides he was going to meet some of Willie's friends. More guys to hang out with his age was a good thing after all. After assessing the situation in his head Thad decided the night would be a good experience for him. He was eager to go out and see some of the nightlife Harlem had to offer.

Chapter 3

After walking down the alley behind Willie's apartment building for a while the boys finally reached the end of the alley. At the end of the alley was an old abandoned building with boarded up windows. Willie walked up to one of the windows and peeked in. "C'mon." he whispered. Willie pulled a board off of the back door and let Thad go in first. The building was dark and dank with a constant cold breeze blowing though it since the air inside couldn't get out. When the two boys got to the front of the old building Thad looked through one of the windows that wasn't boarded upAll he could see were either abandoned or dilapidated buildings. A few of the buildings were still habitable. There was no one outside or any cars driving down the street. There were a few street lights working but they were far and few in between. Willie walked over to a door in a room right off of the main hallway. "Hey Thad. Over here." he said. Thad followed him over to the door and onto the side of the building. When they got outside Thad took another look around the surrounding area.

"C'mon," Willie said "we still got a few blocks to go 'til we there." Although most of them were in decay, Thad still marveled at how many buildings there were in the area. When the boys got to the corner there was another street of mostly vacant buildings. A few people were standing around outside. They were mostly in front of the buildings that people clearly still lived in. Willie led Thad down the street to one of the buildings that looked to be in the same condition as most of the other buildings. Old and rundown with not much to look at.

As they walked around to the side of the building Willie pulled a few dollars out of his pocket. There was a door in the back of the building with a slit at the top for someone to look through. Willie turned to Thad, "Stand up against that wall until they open up." he said. Thad walked over to the wall and stood up against it. Willie walked up to the door with the money in his hand and knocked. The small slit opened and Willie stepped back. The slit closed and the door opened up. Behind the door stood a large man with a bald head, a dark purple suit, and dark sunglasses. He opened up his hand and Willie handed him the money.

Willie walked in with Thad following right behind him. The door closed and the man pointed down the hallway towards a set of stairs that led them upstairs. As Thad and Willie got further up the stairs Thad began to hear music in the distance that grew louder and louder with each step. When Willie opened the door at the top of the steps the mixture of alcohol and smoke filled the entire hall. Every room upstairs was full of teenagers drinking, smoking, dancing, and enjoying themselves. Thad stood behind Willie as he was left in awe at the sight of free living teenagers.

Across the room on a makeshift bandstand was a group of guys playing instruments. None of them looked a day over twenty years old. One kid had a sax, another had a trumpet while the other was on drums. Willie turned to Thad, "You go sit down over there, I'll be back." he said. Thad found a seat at an empty table. A few moments later Willie came back with two huge glass mugs filled with beer. "Here, drink this." he said. "Donny and Chaz ain't make it yet."

"What is it?" Thad asked.

"Beer. A few more and you'll be buzzed."

"It stinks." Thad said. "I don't want it."

"Just drink it."

Thad stared at the beer for a second before taking a few sips. It was bitter and had a bad aftertaste to it. "At least it's cold." he thought to himself. Willie looked up and flagged down two guys who were making their way through the crowd. One was a light skinned black kid and the other was white. When they made it over to the table Willie stood up and gave both of them a dap. The lighter one looked at Thad, "This yo cousin?" he said. "Yeah, this is Thad. Thad this is Donny and Chaz."

Chaz was tall and had a bright skin tone. He had black hair with light brown eyes and always kept waves in his hair. Chaz was arrogant and a real ladies man. His birth name was Charles but he the nickname Chaz because it rhymed with Jazz. Chaz felt that Jazz was the "cool people's music". Since he thought he was the coolest cat in Harlem he chose the nickname Chaz. Donny had a more laid back personality. His parents were immigrants from Ireland. They were a working class family that taught him and his older brother what it meant to work for a living. Donny's older brother Frankie preferred stealing cars and running numbers. It was more exciting than slaving away in a factory and Donny felt the same.

"I see zoots don't exist down south." Chaz joked.

"Huh?" Thad was confused.

"He said you don't have on a suit." Donny said. "Don't mind him, he's already drunk." Thad took another swig from the ice cold mug that was still in his hand.

"How many foxes we gettin tonight?" Chaz said with a slight grin.

"Tonight is just a chill night." Willie said.

"Man yall cats ain't ready to go out on this dance floor and cut a rug with some of these fine ladies? Yall some queers or somethin?" Chaz had his mind set on one thing and one thing only, trying to get one of those girls on that dance floor to go all the way with him. That was his mission every night and he usually succeeded. "Ima dance with one but I ain't in it for what you in it for." Willie said. Chaz started snapping his fingers with the beat as he waltzed around the room looking for a dance partner. Willie grabbed the first girl he saw and started dancing with her. Donny and Thad sat at the table watching everyone else dance. "I'll be back," Donny said "goin to get more beers." Thad was nowhere near finishing his first one. He decided to drink it as fast as he could.

He braced himself and began to chug the ice cold alcoholic beverage. When he finished it the taste just sat at the back of his tongue. "God this is awful." he thought to himself. When he looked down at the table he saw everyone else had already finished their drinks. When Donny came back he had two more mugs of beer in his hands. "I got two more comin'." he said before walking off again. Thad took one of the beers and stared at it for a while. The taste was unbearable but he was growing anxious to see what it felt like to be drunk. "Why not get drunk on a night like tonight?" he thought to himself.

When Donny got back to the table he was visibly drunker than he was before. He was finishing one beer while holding another. When Willie got back he grabbed the vacant beer off of the table and started to drink it. Thad leaned back in his chair and continued to sip his second beer of the night. He was finally beginning to loosen up and enjoying himself. It was his first time being out drinking and it was happening as he listened to live Jazz in New York City. Thad shifted his attention back to the bandstand and the band who were now in full swing. While Donny focused on the music and Willie went off dancing again, Thad noticed a girl standing in the corner all alone. She was very petite with dark brown skin and long black hair. She caught Thad staring at her and blushed a bit before looking away. He didn't know what to do as he froze up. For a second he wanted to look away, the next he wanted to get up and talk to her. He was nervous and completely smitten by her bright and beautiful smile. Donny leaned over towards Thad, "I think you should ask her for a dance." he said. The mix of alcohol and butterflies made it hard for Thad to stand up. He took the oversized glass mug and chugged the last of his beer before standing up and approaching the girl. She noticed his effort and trying to hide her smile.

"Hey, I'm Thaddeus." he said while reached out for her hand. "May I?" The girl gave Thad her hand and the two began to dance. To Thad, he had found the prettiest girl in all of Harlem his first night out, and she was all his for that moment. The city girls in Alabama were pretty, but not like her. She had a glow to her that was so radiant all Thad could do was smile and hope not to do anything stupid like trip and knock her over. The smell of her perfume was as intoxicating as Thad's two mugs of beer. After dancing for a few songs, Thad and his beautiful dance partner sat down at an empty table.

"You a pretty good dancer for a country boy." the girl said.

"How'd you know I was from the country?"

"Well let's see." The girl began to run down the list of qualifications Thad had exhibited during their dance. "Number one you sound like it, number two you dress like it, and number three you act like it."

"How so?"

"First off gentlemen don't exist up here and secondly you don't look like you've ever been to this type of party before."

"That's because I haven't. What's your name?"

"Ashley." the girl replied.

"You here alone?"

"No, my friend left me here to go and dance with that light skinned boy." Thad looked over and saw Ashley's friend dancing with Chaz.

"Oh him," he said "that's Chaz. He's my cousin's friend.

"So Thad, where you from?"

"A small place called Beloit. Ever heard of it?"

"Can't say I have. Where is it?"

"Alabama."

"What you doin all the way up here?"

"I'm here to visit my cousin. You live around here?"

"Yeah, I live in East Harlem."

"Cool. Maybe I'll get to see you again before I leave then" he said. "Who knows." Ashley replied. She touched Thad's hand before she got up and walked away. Thad watched her walk until the crowd enveloped her. Thad wasn't in love but he knew he wanted to see Ashley at least one more time before he left.

Unknown to everyone at the party there was a sudden commotion downstairs. The music was so loud no one could really hear it. Thad was trying to get his eyes to regain focus. That much beer for a lightweight put him over his limit. Out the corner of his eye Thad could see someone making their way to the middle of the packed and busy room. He was shouting something but no one could hear him over the music. He grabbed the guy with the sax and whispered something in his ear. "The pigs is all over the place. Everybody get the hell outta here." The panic swept through the room quicker than a tornado on the Oklahoma plains. Danny and Chaz ran towards the door with the rest of the party goers. Willie grabbed Thad and led him to a closet out in the hall. From inside of the closet all they could hear were countless other teenagers scrambling around on the other side of the door. When the police made their way upstairs they started grabbing everyone they could. While the cops were busy Willie and Thad jumped out of the closet and ran down the stairs.

Thad was panicked, "What we gon do?"

"This way." Willie said. He led Thad to the front of the abandoned house. There were at least four or five squad cars all parked outside causing Willie chang his direction. "This way." he said. The boys ran to the back of the house but had nowhere to go. Just when Willie noticed one of the side rooms, he quickly sprinted over to it and peeked inside. It was empty. Upstairs was still full of commotion as some of the kids began to fight with the police. Thad saw a flashlight glaring down the hall. "Willie." he whispered in a panic. "Willie I think a cop is comin'." Willie looked around the room and saw a window. The only hope he and Thad had of escaping was through that window. "Close the door." Willie said. Thad softly closed the door. Willie opened the window and climbed out. When he got outside he turned around and signaled Thad to climb out next. When Thad got outside the two cousins started to make their way across the street. When they looked back there were kids all over the place. Some were wrestling with police, others were running away from them, and a few were unlucky enough to be in the back of squad cars.

"What just happened?" Thad said.

"Party got raided. That happens a lot around here."

"Why'd you take me if you knew it would get raided?"

"I didn't know one was gon happen tonight," Willie said "besides we got away anyway." Right when Willie said that a voice rang out, "Hey, you two. Stop right now and come here." "Oh shit," yelled Willie "run!" He and Thad took off down the street. On one of the side streets they passed up on their way to the party there was an old and vacant drug store. Willie grabbed Thad and hid beside it. The officer ran past them while still yelling for them stop. "C'mon, we can hide in here for a while 'til the heat die down." Willie said. He picked the lock to the front door and the two slipped in. Willie led Thad to the counter and told him to duck down behind it. Then Willie went back to the front door and locked it from the inside. He walked back to the counter and joined Thad.

"You alright?" Willie asked.

"Yeah, just out of breath. How we gettin' home?"

"Just gotta wait for a minute. Everything should be clear in a bit."

"What about Chaz and Donny?"

"I hope they made it out. They both been arrested before so if they didn't make it ain't no big deal."

It took a while for what Willie said to set in before Thad realized it. "What you mean they been arrested before?" Thad had never heard of someone his age going to jail. "They been to jail. What else you need to know?" Willie said. Suddenly the front door handle began to jiggle. "Shhh." Willie whispered. He stood up to a crouching position and led Thad towards the back to an old storage room. "Shit, it need a key to unlock." Unless there was a spare key in the room, Thad and Willie were trapped. "One thing to do" he said' "we gotta kick the door down and run." Willie began kicking the door which alerted the policemen outside. The harder Willie kicked the harder the cops tried to get in. Then there was a loud crashing sound. The cops had busted through the front window. "In the back." one of them yelled. Just then Willie got the door open and took off running with Thad right behind him. The cops had no chance of catching them now.

When the two got far enough they stopped running. Thad was full of adrenaline. He had never run from the police until then. Of course if he ran from the police back home it was probably for his life. The night was full of firsts for the usually quiet and reserved fourteen year old. "We'll take the side streets back. Cops like to sit in alleys around here." Willie said. On the way back home Thad could see lights shining up in the air.

"Where those light comin' from?" he said.

"Some of the clubs that's still open." Willie

answered. The lights were shining so brightly into the air that Thad couldn't even see the stars. Back home in Alabama stars lit up the night sky. All Thad could hear was a bunch of instruments all playing different songs. He was so drunk earlier he didn't even get to enjoy the music at the party. Then he realized he wasn't as drunk anymore. "Hey Willie," he said "why was I drunk earlier but now I'm not?"

"You still is, but that runnin' from the police got you thinkin' different." he said

"Were you drunk?"

"Naw. You just a lightweight."

Thad began to notice the sudden change in scenery again. The bright lights from the next street over were beginning to be fade away. The only light that was shining now were the dim and barely lit streetlights. Through the entire night he realized Willie had a calm demeanor, he hardly panicked or broke a sweat the entire night. "How Willie stay calm the entire night?" Thad thought. Willie was a street smart city kid from Harlem who was used to these kinds of things. When Thad finally thought about it, the night could have ended terribly. They could be sitting in a jail cell waiting on Aunt Bird, but they weren't. Although they managed to get away, this was not the experience Thad was hoping for on his first night in Harlem. He wanted to tell Willie that he was done with sneaking out late and getting into trouble, but he didn't know how. "Maybe I'll tell him tomorrow." he thought to himself. "Or I could tell him tonight so I can have a clear head in the morning." He wasn't sure how or when to tell Willie, but he definitely was done with sneaking out and going to parties.

When they got home Willie stopped Thad to give him a rundown of the procedures in which to sneak back into the apartment. "Listen, walk as light as you can up the fire escape. When you get up there take ya shoes off at the door. Got it?" Thad shook his head yes. "Good," said Willie "I'll go up first." Willie jumped up and grabbed the ladder. After pulling himself up he slowly let the ladder down in order to keep it quiet and not wake up any neighbors. Thad climbed up next. When they got upstairs Thad did everything Willie told him to do. When he got into the room Thad laid down on the bed. He was exhausted and sleepy. All he kept thinking about was how close he and Willie had been to being arrested. Then he remembered what Willie said about Chaz and Donny both being arrested. "Wonder what they did." Thad .

The fact that Willie hung out with those kinds of kids made Thad suspicious. He had always wanted to meet his cousin Willie. He was the son of his mother's older sister, why wouldn't he want to meet him? The only problem was he didn't know what type of kid Willie truly was. After the night had ended Thad had a pretty good idea. He started to wonder if Willie had ever been to jail himself. Thad was pretty sure he had been. If Thad joined Willie on every one of his wild excursions, Thad was sure to end up there too and Thad's vacation would turn into a nightmare. He decided he had to tell Willie not to include him in any more of his late night plans.

Thad walked into the living room where Willie was. He leaned over and saw Willie's eyes were closed. He wanted to wake him up but decided it wasn't the right time. As he walked away Willie opened his eyes. "You wanted somethin'?" he tiredly asked. Thad turned around. He was a little nervous since he didn't know how Willie would react.

"Yeah I did. Tonight was fun and all but I don't think I wanna be in that type of a situation again." Thad stood there looking at the back of the couch that had Willie's leg draped over the it. "Alright" Willie said in a calm manner. Thad was shocked. He wasn't expecting that answer. "So I guess I'll see you in the morning." he said. "Goodnight." Willie didn't respond. He was fast asleep. Thad walked back to Willie's room and closed the door. He turned off the light and laid down. His first night in Harlem was an eventful one. As Thad began to fall asleep all he could think of was Ashley. Now that he saw her and knew she existed he was smitten. "If I get another chance," he thought to himself "I'm gonna kiss that girl." With the police chase, wild party behind him, and his peace of mind Thad slowly drifted off to sleep.

Chapter 4

When Thad woke up the next morning the collar of his t shirt was damp with sweat. His head was relentlessly pounding as the sun shined into the hot and humid room. He wasn't sure if everything that had happened the night before was all a dream or if it had actually happened. He looked across the room and saw his clothes he had worn to the party sitting in the chair. "At least I'm not in jail." he whispered to himself. With a pounding headache and exhausted body, Thad laid back down and closed his eyes in hopes of getting some more sleep. As his eyes began to shut there were two small knocks at the door. Before he could get the energy to sit up and respond Daisy poked her head into the room.

"You awake?" she asked.

"I am now. What's up?"

"Nothin'. My mommy cookin' us breakfast, want some?"

"Sure." he said. Daisy closed the door as her small footsteps moved down the hallway and towards the kitchen. Since Thad found himself up and unable to go back to sleep he decided to get up and take a bath. After he got dressed Thad went into the living room to lay down. He noticed Willie was sitting and listening to the radio with a glass of orange juice next to him. "You finally up I see." he said. Thad didn't respond. After allowing last night's events to soak in Thad was a little upset with Willie for taking him to the party. "So we not speakin' this mornin' huh?" Willie teased. "Ok then." Willie continued to listen to the radio as if Thad had never walked in. When Thad got up and went into the kitchen he was glad to see Aunt Bird.

"Good morning Thad." she said. "Hope you slept good."

"I slept ok." he said.

"That's good. Well you came in at the right time. I made pancakes, some with blueberries. I wasn't sure if you liked blueberries or not, and I made bacon and eggs. Sounds good?"

"Yeah it sounds great." he said. For the moment, the large breakfast Aunt Bird had made was enough to take Thad's mind off of how upset he was with Willie about last night. When Thad sat down the girls were arguing

over which one of them did a better job of setting the
table. As Thad sat there at the table he began to remember
everything from the previous night. The walk to the old
building, the music and the atmosphere, then he
remembered the girl with the pretty smile and caramel
colored skin. "What was her name?" he thought to
himself. He thought on it for a brief moment upsetting
himself when he failed to remember. All Thad could think
of was him and Willie almost being arrested. "Maybe I'm
overreacting." he thought to himself. "Willie, food's
done." Aunt Bird yelled down the hall. The radio turned
off and Willie came into the kitchen.

When Willie sat next to him Thad was hoping there
wouldn't be any awkward tension between him and
Willie. Thad didn't mean to give Willie the cold shoulder.
He was just shaken up about what had happened.
Everyone at the table sat and ate in silence until Daisy
finally broke the ice.

"This is good mommy." she said.

"Thank you." Aunt Bird said with her bright smile.
She turned her attention to Willie and Thad. "So what did
you two do last night?"

All Thad could think about was the smell of alcohol in the air, flashing police lights, and a congregation of teenagers running in all different directions fearing being hauled away. He couldn't tell Aunt Bird about that. Thad could feel his heart in his throat, he had no idea of what to say. Thad tried to think of a simple little lie but nothing came to his mind.

Thad was usually a pretty honest kid. One day when he was in the sixth grade Thad had skipped a day at school. He and a couple of his friends decided to go to a small lake nearby for a swim. When Thad and his friends never showed up to school his teacher grew concerned. At lunch his teacher called his grandmother to tell her that Thad hadn't come to school that day. Not knowing where he had gone she became worried. Later that evening as the sun began to go down Thad finally made his way back home where his grandmother was waiting on him. When Thad saw her with a switch in her hand she had ripped down from a tree outside he knew he was in trouble. "I want the truth now," she said while waving the switch "why did you skip school? Nobody knew where you were. If it wasn't for Thomas' mother we would've had to call a search party." Ever since that day Thad remembered the importance of the truth.

With Thad still frozen Willie finally spoke up. "We just sat around all night listenin' to music talkin' for a minute until we got tired. Hey Thad," Willie said while turning to face him, "didn't I fall asleep before you?" he said.

Thad stopped eating his breakfast and looked Aunt Bird dead in her eye, "Yeah that was pretty much all we did." he said before going back to eating. "That was a bended truth but it wasn't a lie." he thought.

"He likes jazz too." Willie added.

Aunt Bird just gave Willie a blank stare, "That's all you did last night?" she said. Thad was expecting Aunt Bird to somehow know that he and Willie had snuck out to go to the party. "What else was it to do last night?" Willie said.

"Well you should take him out to see some more of the city." Aunt Bird said. Thad felt the weight of the world lift off of his shoulders. Willie had told Aunt Bird all she needed to hear about last night. They listened to Jazz and talked for a bit. When they were tired Willie did

in fact fall asleep before Thad did. Willie gave Thad a
quick glance and a smirk.

When everyone was finished eating breakfast Aunt
Bird asked the girls to help her clean the kitchen. Willie
placed his plate in the sink and went back into the living
room. Thad felt bad about not speaking to Willie earlier
that morning. "All he wanted to do was show me a good
time my first night here." he thought. He set his plate in
the sink and went into the living room. He decided the
best thing for him to do was apologize to Willie, but when
he got to the living room Willie had already left. Thad sat
down on the couch and turned the radio on. A few
moments later Denise walked in and sat down.

"What you doin?" she said.

"Nothin'."

"Why you look that?"

"Like what?" Thad said.

"Like you stole some money or somethin. Trust me"
she said "I know what that face look like." He sat up and
fixed his face. There was no sense in moping around all
day. It wasn't like Willie yelled at him or got upset. All
Thad could do was wait until Willie got back to

apologize. Besides, if an eight year old can see that you're upset then you should fix your face. "I'm just tired." he said. Denise gave Thad a slight scowl. "Now I done been sleepy, and I done stole money, and you look like you stole money." she said.

"You are one persistent little girl." Thad said. Denise was a very quick witted kid. She had a smart and sassy mouth that she probably got from her brother. Her favorite thing to do was challenge authority. With as bright a mind as hers that wasn't hard to do. Since Thad was older and she didn't know him too well, it only felt right for her to push his buttons. "What's persistent?" she said.

"It means you don't let people be when they want to be left alone". Thad refused to allow an eight year old verbally push him around. "So If you would, can I get some peace to myself?" he said.

"You borin' anyway." Denise stood up and walked out of the room. Although she was a rather minute distraction Thad was happy Daisy had finally left. Thad decided it was the perfect time to catch himself a quick cat nap. He kicked off his shoes and laid down on the couch. When he woke Thad could tell it was a little later in the day. When he sat up there was laughter coming from the kitchen. He rubbed his eyes and got up to go see what was going on. Willie was playing cards with his sisters. Thad sat down at the table and watched. "Wanna play?" Daisy said. "Naw, I'm ok." Willie continued to play cards with the girls for a few more games as Thad watched. When they were done playing the final game Thad asked Willie if he could talk to him for a second. Willie agreed and the two went into the living room.

"Sorry for the cold shoulder thing earlier. I just wasn't expecting all of that to happen last night" he said.

"It's alright man. I saw you was a lil' shook up about it, so I let you breathe. Look, no more parties like that. We can find other shit around here to do."

"Thanks for understandin' where I'm comin from. So what you plan on doin' today?"

"I gotta go do somethin' right now but I'll be back in a few." Before heading to the front door Willie turned around and looked at Thad, "Hey do me a favor, keep my sisters occupied." he said. Willie walked out closing the door behind him. Thad sat down on the couch and

wondered where Willie was headed. A few moments later
Aunt Bird reemerged from her room after taking her daily
nap in between her motherly duties.

"Where's Willie?" she said.

"He just left out."

"Probably up to no good as usual." she said. "I wish I
knew a way to keep him out of these streets." She shook
her head in disappointment then walked down the hall
towards the kitchen. Thad sat on the couch and looked out
the window. Standing on the corner was a man who
looked no older than his early twenties with a saxophone
in his hand. Thad found it a little strange for him to not be
carrying it in a case. His suit was a dirty and he wasn't
well kept. Thad shifted all of his attention to the young
musician. When the man started to play Thad heard one
of the most beautiful melodies he had ever heard. Every
note seemed to link together just perfectly like a beautiful
gold link chain. It was like watching an elderly woman
sew a long beautiful cashmere scarf. Thad's ears and soul
were enslaved by the music. The only person he heard
play this well in person was Catfish, and that was the first
time Thad ever heard someone play Jazz in person. "If I

could learn to play like that, I'd shock the world." he thought to himself.

As the young man continued to play Thad realized people who walked past him were placing money into the young musician's hat as they passed him by. They weren't giving him bills, they were just merely throwing change into the hat. This confused Thad. Here was a young musician who was playing some of the most beautiful music he had ever heard, and people were paying him nickels and dimes. "He should be selling out clubs and concerts hall." he thought. After watching and listening to the young musician play for almost an hour Thad watched the musician pick up his hat, count the change he had earned, then walk away. Thad wasn't sure what was going on but he did know that besides the beautiful music this was not a happy occasion. Thad got up and went into the kitchen where Aunt Bird was reading with the girls. He could hear them bickering before he reached the end of the hall.

"You read my part." "No I didn't." Thad couldn't tell one high pitched voice from the other. "Ok girls, I think that's enough. Hey Thad." Aunt Bird said after Thad made his way into the kitchen. "I've been meaning to speak to you. Girls, go play." Daisy and Denise sprang up and went to the front room. When she knew the girls were gone Aunt Bird asked Thad to sit down. "Thad, I wanna be honest with you," she said "I know you and Willie are getting along and I like that. Just please do me one favor," She took a pause "don't allow Willie to get you into any trouble while you're up here. He's my son and I love him, but he has a problem of running in the streets."

"I understand." Thad said. He knew Aunt Bird was serious, or else the girls would have been allowed to stay in the room. "Ever since my husband died Willie's been in and out of juvenile centers and he rarely goes to school. This is the longest stretch he's been home in a while." Aunt Bird stopped to collect herself. "But I'm glad you came to visit us. I'm gonna get dinner started in a few. You go and keep the girls some company." Thad went into the living room where Denise and Daisy were listening to the radio.

"So what you guys up to?" Thad asked while walking into the room.

"Just listenin' to music." Daisy said. "Why come you

don't play with me and Denise?"

"I haven't had the chance to."

"Well, you not doin nothin' now. Wanna play with us?" Daisy asked.

"Sure. What ya'll wanna play?"

"I don't know. Denise what you wanna play?"

Denise turned her face up and thought as hard as she could. "I got nothin'" she said.

"How can we play if nobody can think of a game?" Thad said. "How about this, we'll just listen to the radio and wait for your mom to finish cookin'. Deal?" Daisy shook her head yes. Denise who still wasn't over what Thad said to her earlier decided to get up and leave.

"Don't mind her, she always got a attitude." Daisy said. Thad really liked Daisy. It was like having a little sister and that made Thad feel at home. Thad was enjoying his time with Daisy so much that he hadn't realized how much time had passed. When Willie walked through the door he looked exhausted. "Daisy go play. I gotta ask Thad somethin'." he said.

"But I was talkin to him." she contested.

"You can talk to him later but for now, go and play."

Daisy got up and stormed out of the room. "I got word of a hangout later on tonight if you wanna come." Thad was weary of going out with Willie. Even more so after Aunt Bird told Thad to be careful about hanging around him.

"I think I'll stay home tonight." he said.

"You sure?"

"Yeah I'm sure."

"Alright then." Willie said. He stood up and walked down the hall. Thad wanted to see more of the city but he didn't want to see it Willie's way. Thad stayed in the living room and turned on the radio. The Yankees were playing Detroit and Thad had never listened to an entire baseball game on the radio before. Listening to the Yankees was a big deal to Thad. They were the greatest ever in his opinion. He decided to kick his feet up and listen to the rest of the game as the announcer celebrated another Yankees homerun.

Chapter 5

A few days later after Thad woke up from a nap he went into the kitchen to get himself a glass of water. There was a pack of cards that was sitting on the kitchen table. He picked up the cards and started to play a game of solitaire. After about his third game, Daisy walked in and sat down at the table while rubbing her eyes. "How you play go fish by yourself?" she said.

"I'm not playin' go fish," Thad answered "I'm playin' solitaire."

"I never played that game."

"Is Aunt Bird up yet?"

"Not yet."

When the front door opened up Thad knew it had to be Willie. A few moments later the bathroom door closed. Aunt Bird came out of her bedroom and knocked on the bathroom door. "Hurry up now," she said "you know I gotta get ready and leave for work in a bit." She walked back into her bedroom and closed the door. Thad went back into the living room as Daisy followed right behind him. Thad sat staring at Daisy as she blankly stared back.

"How long you gon be here?" she asked.

"Three weeks," Thad replied.

"Do you listen to the radio this much at home?"

"Sometimes if I have nothin' to do."

"So you bored of bein' here?"

"No, why'd you ask that?"

"Because, you said you listen to the radio this much when you have nothin' to do, that means you're bored."

"I guess you're right. What do you do for fun besides ask me a bunch of questions?" Thad wanted his question to get Daisy busy for a moment until he though up what to say to Willie. Just as hard as Thad was thinking so was Daisy who still hadn't come up with an answer.

"Well," she said "I like to play go fish and old maid, play with my dolls, and go to Alisha's house."

Thad's simple mind trick had failed. He had to buy more time before Willie came out of the bathroom. He had to think fast. "Who's that?" he said.

"Me and Denise's friend. She lives a floor under us."

The easiest thing for him to do was to keep rattling off questions. "How often you go down there?"

"I don't know. Why you keep askin' so many

questions?" Daisey asked.

"You just asked me a bunch of questions, why can't I ask you a bunch of questions?"

"I'm a kid, kids ask a lot of questions"

Denise walked in as Thad and Daisy turned looking in her direction. "What, yall was waitin' on me or somethin'?" she said. "Girl you ain't nobody special." a voice rang out. It was Willie who was standing right behind her. "Go and get whatever you takin' down there." he said. Willie sat down on the couch and leaned his head back, he looked as though he had just worked an eight hour shift at a factory. Thad sat there and looked at Willie. Willie didn't move or open his eyes once. "Ay." he finally said, "I'm headed outside to go hang out with some of the fellas, wanna come?" Thad wasn't too sure about the company Willie liked to surround himself with.

"Where we goin" he asked . "Just around to the back of the building." Thad took a moment to think about it. There wasn't too much trouble he and Willie could get into by going to the back of the building. Besides, the interior of the apartment was beginning to bore Thad. "Sure, I'll go." he said. Willie went to his room and grabbed some money before heading out the door. When Thad and Willie reached the end of the hall they waited on the elevator which had finally been fixed after a group of tenants called the building manager complaining about it being down for so long. They stood in the elevator in silence until Willie finally said something. "I better win some money today." he said.

"Money doing what?" Thad asked.

"Money off this craps game. Ima bust they ass, just watch." Willie said. "These niggas gon' see all naturals off this wrist."

When they got off the elevator Willie led Thad down the left side of the building. Thad could already hear some chatter. When Willie and Thad made it to the back Thad found a spot to sit and watch the game. There was a group of guys huddled in one area up against the wall. They threw the dice up against the wall hoping to hit their points and collect the pot. All of the guys were in Willie and Thad's age range. Chaz was the loudest of them all. He was the type of person you heard before you saw him.

Then there was Dino and a couple of his boys. Thad remembered his face from his first day in Harlem. They were from a small gang who fought Hispanics and other kids in nearby neighborhoods. Dino was one of the toughest kids around. He also found himself in the most trouble. Dino was known for owning multiple guns and not being afraid to use any them. He did stick ups and had shoot outs with rivals or the police. One time he shot out with both. The fact that Dino kept avoiding jail amazed everyone who knew him because he was such a loose cannon. He respected Willie because Willie didn't take a bunch of shit from people.

"Time to show you how I do these niggas up here in Harlem Thad." Willie bragged.

"Shut ya black ass up and roll nigga." said Chaz. Willie picked up the dice and rolled them against the wall. "Seven!" he yelled. Willie collected his earnings and rolled again. Everyone in the circle had money whether it was on the ground, in their hands, or under their shoes. A couple of the guys were smoking cigarettes and a few were smoking the stuff Thad smelled at the party. He didn't know what it was but it definitely was not cigarette smoke. "Lets see eleven." Willie said. Willie rolled a five, "I got the nine five." yelled one of the guys in the circle. Another kid put a few bucks down with him. Willie rolled an eight. Dino held out an extra dollar. Willie looked at him then threw out another dollar. He picked up the dice and rolled them again. This time he rolled a seven. "Damn!" he yelled out. Dino picked up the money and snickered. "Damn Willie, where the natural wrist?" Dino joked.

"Just had a unlucky roll." Willie walked over to where Thad was sitting and took a seat next to him.

"I ain't wanna gamble too much," he said "need money for the rest of the week."

"I never watched a craps game before." Thad said.

"This is all we do up here."

Willie and Thad sat and watched the dice game while they talked to eachother. As the dice rolled the money continued to exchanged hands and the bottom of soles as the profanity laced dialogue continued to fly. "I ain't have half the bank yall niggas had when I got here. And a hour later all yall niggas broke." Chaz said.

"Shut yo high yellow ass up." one of the guys in the huddle said.

"Look man," said Chaz "if yall got just a lil bit, just a

whiff of pussy, you can have a wrist like me." Chaz looked at Willie, "This move right here Willie." he said. Chaz was gyrating his hips as if he were with a girl.

Thad turned to Willie, "Chaz is the biggest shit talker I have ever met." he said.

"Yeah. That's Chaz though." Willie said.

"Where's Donny?"

"Who knows, his brother probably got him ridin' around with him."

"I been meaning to ask you a question." Thad said. "What's up?" Suddenly Dino yelled. "Re-roll nigga". Another kid by the name of Reg was looking at Dino.

"Naw man, that was my point." he said.

"It don't read."

"Shit, why don't it?"

"It landed in a crack. You know that don't read." Two of Dino's friends who had been watching the dispute gradually unfold stood up and walked over towards Dino. "Dino you ain't gotta take that shit." one of them instigated. "I don't care what none of yall niggas say, I hit my point. Now gimme my money." he said. Reg was fuming with anger. Dino looked at his boys then turned back around and looked at Reg. He threw the money on the ground then looked at Reg. "Pick it up then nigga." Reg looked at the money then looked back at Willie. "I ain't pickin' up shit." Reg yelled. "Did he just raise his voice at me?" Dino said sarcastically. Dino's friends made their way towards Reg. "I know this nigga did not just raise his voice at me." Chaz stepped between Dino and Reg in an attempt to diffuse the situation. "Aye man, yall niggas chill out." he said. "This just a game."

"Dino, Ima ask you one more time, gimme my money."

"Or what Reg? What yo punk ass gon' do?"

"Ima beat yo ass!" Reg took off his Jacket and threw it down. He rolled up his sleeves and stepped up to Dino. Dino looked at the jacket then looked at Reg.

Chaz stepped between Dino and Reg again, "Aye man yall niggas chill out" he said, "this just a dice game." Neither Reg nor Dino showed any intent of backing down.

"Dino, Ima ask one more time, gimme my money" he said. Dino walked over to Reg and looked him in his eye, "Or what Reg? What yo punk ass gon do nigga?"

"Ima beat yo ass like I said." Reg took a step back. He was standing as if he was challenging Dino to a fight. Willie grabbed Thad by the arm. "Let's go." he said. Everyone else stayed to watch what happened next. Willie led Thad back into the building as fast as he could. Willie had a concerned look on his face. When the elevator got to the first floor he and Thad slowly walked onto the elevator. Suddenly there were three loud pops that came from outside. The shots made Thad and Willie jump. When they got to Willie's floor the boys heard a woman yelling as a man's voice rang out, "Somebody call the police!"

Before the both of them could even walk into the apartment Aunt Bird came running down the hall, "What was that?" she said.

"I think they were gunshots." Thad said

"Did somebody get shot?"

"I hope not." Willie said.

Aunt Bird walked over to the window and looked down at the street. The corner in front of the Noble Veronica was full of people looking around and talking. "I think you all should stay in here for the rest of the day.

This neighborhood is not what it used to be." she said. Aunt Bird walked back towards the kitchen shaking her head. When he was sure Aunt Bird was back in the kitchen, Thad sat down on the couch next to Willie. "Did Dino-" Willie looked up, "I know he did." he said. When Thad and Willie heard the sirens they walked over to the window and looked down at the street. There were police cars and an ambulance pulling up. As Thad looked around he could see people peeking out of their windows. A few people were even sitting in their windows. Aunt Bird came walking out of the kitchen to look through the window again. "I just can't believe this. This is not the Harlem I moved to twenty years ago."

Thad stood at the window watching as the events unfolded. From the police questioning the people standing on the street to when the detectives arrived. When Thad saw Reg's body getting put in the back of the ambulance wrapped in a sheet the reality of the situation hit him. "What a trip this is turning out to be." he thought.

Later that evening as Aunt Bird grabbed her things to go and start her shift she pulled Willie to the side and went down a list of things she wanted him to do that night. When she was done she said goodbye then headed out the door. Thad was in his now usual spot in the living room listening to the radio. The girls had finally come home after being at their friend's house playing for most of the day. Denise sat down on the couch across from where Thad was sitting. "I heard they was shootin' today. You heard it?" Thad didn't want to talk about it. Denise's excitement disturbed Thad. "Me and Willie heard the shots." he said.

"Man I wonder if somebody got shot. That'll be crazy." Denise jumped off the couch and went into her mother's room.

Thad walked into the kitchen where Willie was on the phone and stirring pasta in a pot. Thad sat down at the table and waited for Willie to get off of the phone. When Willie hung up he had a huge smile on his face. He turned around and looked at Thad. "Aye man," he said "I got this broad across the way who want me to come over, think you could do me a favor tonight?"

"How big is the favor?" Thad said.

"Not too big. Just watch my sisters and send 'em to bed. I'll be gone for like a hour. That's all."

"Sure." Thad said "I can do that. And you'll only be gone an hour?" he said.

"Yeah man, Be back around ten."

"So What's for dinner?"

"Spaghetti. My mom made the sauce already so just help yaself."

Willie called the girls in to eat. "I'm goin' to do somethin for mom real quick. I'll be back but you'll probably be sleep."

"So Thad is watchin' us?" Daisy said.

"Yeah, so be good. And go to bed when he says." Willie gave both of his sisters a kiss on the forehead and headed out the front door. Thad didn't know what to do when babysitting. He had never watched two little girls before. He sat them down and made them both a bowl of spaghetti. "Can we eat in the living room and listen to Captain Buck?" Daisy said.

"Sure." The three of them went into the living room and sat down. Denise changed the station to Captain Buck. "What is this program about?"

"It's about a captain who got stranded on Mars and found out Martians are real." Daisy said. "So the Martians

help Captain Buck fix his ship while he protect them."
Denise added. The program's theme song came on as the
narrator set the stage for the opening scene. Thad sat and
listened to the entire program with the girls. It too his
mind off of everything he had experienced over the past
couple of days. When the girl's program was over he had
to figure out how to keep them entertained for another
thirty minutes. He decided to play cards with them since
that was one of their favorite things to do.

"Yall wanna play go fish or old maid?" Thad said.

"I want cake." Denise said.

"Me too." Daisy added. Thad got up and cut the girls
each a slice of cake. When the girls were done eating their
cake Thad sent them to bed. He got them dressed and
made them brush their teeth like his grandmother made
him do when he was their age. After he put them to bed
Thad realized his entire night was spent taking care of
Willie's sisters. Although spending time with the girls
was fun, he didn't like being confined to the apartment.
He realized there was no reason to get upset. Thad did
enjoy listening to Captain Buck with the girls and it was
better than running from police through old abandoned

buildings. Thad went into Willie's room to lay down. He began to doze off when he heard the back door open. He knew it was Willie coming back from wherever he had been that night. Thad got up and went into the kitchen where Willie was fixing himself a plate.

"Hey," Thad said "you made it on time."

"Yeah, the girls sleep yet?"

"They should be." Thad said. "Willie I got a question. Is what happened today normal? Does that happen a lot around here?"

"What, the dice game or somebody gettin' killed?"

"Seeing Reg get taken away on a stretcher was..." Thad didn't know what he wanted to say.

"It's just everyday life to me. Don't get too caught up on it."

"All I can see is his face."

"Mourn him then forget." Willie said. "He ain't the first and he ain't the last."

"I'm just not used to seeing this kind of stuff. You hear about it but you never actually see it."

Thad couldn't comprehend the Harlem way of living. He was used to a quiet small town in rural Alabama, not this fast bustling metropolitan lifestyle. What Thad really wanted to know was how does a young man escape the daily occurrences of the city. Sure Alabama had its own problems with racism and violence but the violence in Harlem just seemed different. "I don't know, this is just life for us I guess." Willie said. To Thad, the north was seen as a "new" America. The north was where you went to get away from all of the segregation and Jim Crowe laws back home. Life was supposed to be simpler. Thad was expecting a different Harlem. A Harlem that was more cultured. All Thad could think about was what the man on the train had told him, and he was right. Harlem wasn't the same. Willie dug into his spaghetti and started to eat.

Later that night as Thad tried to get some sleep, he kept thinking about Reg. The sound of the gunshots echoed in his head like a record on repeat as Reg's face kept appearing in his thoughts. Seeing one of his peers gunned down over a craps game had shaken him up. As he laid in bed Thad could hear a saxophone playing. He looked out the window and saw the same guy on the corner from the night before. Thad sat up and listened to the dirty and un-kept man play for a bit. To Thad the one jewel the former black utopia had left was it's Jazz.

Chapter 6

Thad's daily routine had become mundane. When he woke up he went into the bathroom to take a bath and brush his teeth. Then he went back into Willie's room to get dressed. The girls would be eating breakfast with Aunt Bird who would always leave a plate out for Thad. Willie would usually already be gone by breakfast. After breakfast Thad would go into the living room and turn on the radio. He would either fall back to sleep or listen to the radio until he fell asleep. The girls either left to go to their friend Alisha's for a few hours or sat around the apartment playing together. Aunt Bird would go into her room and catch up on some sleep after getting off of the late shift.

After being in Harlem for a week Thad was becoming bored with the same old routine day in and day out. At least when he was bored back home he had some friends to be bored with. Sitting in that two bedroom apartment all day felt more like a jail sentence than a vacation. If there was anyone that could save him from this boredom it was Willie. Being chased by the cops was more exciting than playing Go Fish with an eight and five year old almost every night. Thad kicked off his shoes and laid down on the couch. He was bored with naps but sleep was the only thing that kept him occupied.

About a half hour later Thad was awakened by the radio. Willie was sitting in the chair listening to the Yankees. "Daily nap?" Willie said.

"Yeah. Hey You doin' anything tonight?"

"Nothin' special, why?"

"I was hopin' you had somethin' to do today. I can't just sit around here all day again. No offense."

"It's too hot to do anything around here right now." Willie said.

"It's not that warm out."

Willie chuckled, "Not weather hot. Hot like the pigs is out. Ever since Reg got shot they been out throwin' niggas in cars for anything. I got stopped last night."

"Oh. So we stuck in here all day?"

"Not necessarily."

Thad sat up on the couch, "If you go anywhere, do anything, I wanna go." he said. Willie nodded and turned the volume on the radio up.

After the game ended Willie and Thad left out. Thad didn't ask any questions. He was just happy to finally get out of the apartment. A few days after the shooting the police couldn't find any leads and decided to tone down their investigation. They realized trying to find out who killed Reg was an almost impossible feat. In an urban community like this one people rarely talked to police or cooperated. Not because they didn't like the police but because they were scared of what might happen to them if they did. Everyone wondered where Dino and his buddies had gone. No one had heard from or seen Dino since the dice game.

Thad and Willie walked for a few blocks while talking about the city. "What was it like when the mobsters were in control?" he said.

"Were?" said Willie. "Shit, them niggas still got a hold on damn near every borough. Instead of booze they mostly got a hand in gambling'. Some sell drugs but that's rare. Somethin' about a code."

"So what's the crime like now, besides what we saw." Thad said.

"Exactly what you saw. Niggas shootin niggas,

robbin stores and what not."

After the boys walked a few blocks they turned around and started to head back home. "I want to see more of Harlem" Thad said. He knew there had to be some nice places he didn't get to see his first night there since they were taking every alley way and side street possible. "I wanna see the strip we ain't get to see last time. I wanna know what an actual Jazz Club looks like." he said

"We live across the street from one."

"Yeah but it's abandoned, that ain't fun to look at. Your whole neighborhood is decayed buildings. I wanna see some that's at least kept up."

"Well it ain't none." Willie said. "Those years is over. Look around, this is Harlem. Take it or leave it."

The long and narrow street that had only two lanes was lined with old closed clubs and businesses with a few tenement buildings. Even some of those were old and run down. There were a few people walking on the sidewalks and a group of young kids walking down the street towards a field with baseball bats and gloves. A few guys who were older than Thad and Willie stood on the corner drinking, smoking and laughing. The street's pavement was crumbled and the sidewalks were cracked. One building had police tape marking it off. "This where I call home." Willie said. Thad looked around and saw a paradise lost. An occasional police siren would blare every once in a while. Thad let out a sigh, "So this is Harlem now." he thought to himself.

When Thad was done sight seeing Willie led them around a corner and started to head back home. Before that moment Thad was expecting to see huge grandiose Jazz clubs the size of European opera houses. Bright lights that shot straight up into the air as rich white people got out of their expensive cars to go inside of those very grandiose clubs. Thad now understood the buildings with the busted windows and missing doors were the ruins of the old Harlem. Bricks had long since fallen out of place and many of the buildings had been boarded up. One building's roof was completely collapsed in. Some buildings had burned mattresses and charred walls covered in black soot. Thad took a long hard look at his surroundings as he sat down on a curb. Willie took a seat beside him.

"I don't know what I was expecting." Thad said. "There was this guy on the train who told me it wasn't the same here. Is the entire city like this?"

"Only certain parts. All of the city can't be lit up with fancy rich white folks. Niggas gotta live somewhere too. We got the ghetto."

After sitting on the curb for a moment Willie stood up dusting off the back of his pants. "C'mon," he said "let's head back to the house."

When they got back home Aunt Bird was hopping down the hall with one shoe. She had picked up a few extra hours of overtime but had overslept. "Willie I got some biscuits in the oven, you can figure out something to do with them" she said. She slipped on her other shoe and grabbed her purse before rushing out of the door.

"Ima call Donny and Chaz and see what they up to tonight." Willie said. "Damn, I gotta go get the girls." Willie rushed out of the door to go get his sitters from their friend's apartment. When Willie got back the girls were lagging behind him with long faces. He led them to the kitchen then came back out to talk to Thad. He peeked around the corner to make sure the girls weren't in the hallway.

"Hey Thad." he said. "Donny got some grass and he wanna come over here with Chaz. You wanna smoke?"

Thad had heard of grass before but he wasn't sure if he and Willie were thinking about the same grass. "Like marijuana grass?" he said.

"Yeah like marijuana grass. I know them country niggas you know be smokin'."

"Yeah but I never tried it."

"Then tonight is the night. We gon get you high as a kite. Let me get the girls to bed then we can get this show rollin'." Thad sat down on the couch and started to wonder what it would feel like to be high. He remembered hearing terrible stories of what can happen to you when you get high. When he saw older guys back home smoking they never had the symptoms old people would exaggerate about. Thad just wanted to experience it for himself. He tried smoking a cigarette once and all it did was made him cough for about fifteen minutes. He was hoping the marijuana wouldn't do the same. A few hours later the girls came into the living room to listen to their favorite radio program, Captain Buck. Thad and

Willie went into Willie's room. The entire time Thad couldn't take his mind off of smoking. "What is it gonna feel like?" he though to himself. "Is it better than drinkin'?" He figured the best way to find out was to ask Willie. "What does bein' high feel like?"

"Man it's a feelin' you can't explain. You feel weightless, almost like you floatin'. But you never leave the ground, and that ain't even the best part. Wait until you get the munchies."

"The munchies?" Thad obliviously asked.

"Yeah, you get real hungry then you eat like you never ate before. Everything tastes good at that point."

"I need those to eat chitlins then." Thad said.

"I don't think you can make those taste good."

When the girls' radio program went off Willie ran them both a bath. When they were all washed up and dressed he put them to bed. Willie and Thad sat in the kitchen and waited for Donny and Chaz. Chaz had moved to Harlem from Greensboro, North Carolina when he was four with his parents, grandmother, and aunt. Donny was from Brooklyn where his parents settled after his brother was born in Ireland. He had to either catch the train to

Harlem or have his brother drop him off. Donny's Brooklyn neighborhood wasn't very black friendly. They weren't very Irish friendly either. Suddenly there was a knock at the back door. " My niggas." Willie said. He jumped up and sprinted towards the door letting Donny and Chaz in. Willie led them to the living room where Thad was sitting. "How much this costin' me," Willie said.

"This time it's free." Donny said. "My brother had a bunch of it. I sold some to the Italian kids on my block and a bunch to the black kids a few blocks over." Thad caught on to conversation quickly. Donny pulled a small metal tin out of his pocket and opened it up. Thad leaned in to look at it. "So that's it right there?" he said.

"Yep. Green dope. Not that brown shit these artistic kids put in their arms."

"Then let's hit the escape and smoke up." Chaz said. Donny got up and headed towards the kitchen first. Thad and Chaz followed with Willie in the back. Willie slipped his head into the door and saw both of his sisters were still sleeping. He followed the guys out onto the fire escape. "Thad should get first hit." Donny suggested. He pulled out a tightly rolled joint and a lighter and handed it to Thad. "Now light it and inhale at the same time while you hit it, like a cigarette." Donny said. Thad put the lighter to the joint and did exactly what Donny told him to. As Thad inhaled he felt as though every bit of air from his lungs had just left his body. "Now hold it." Willie said. Thad held it for a few seconds then exhaled. When he exhaled he let out a huge cough. "One more." Willie said while laughing. Thad hit the joint a second time. When he exhaled again he let out another loud and bellowing cough. "I gotta sit down," he said.

All of the boys started to laugh. "He did better than Willie did." Chaz said. "Remember that Donny? Back in what was it, eighth grade? We ain't think he was gon make it."

"And how was your first time," Willie asked. "From what I remember you almost cried"

"My throat hurt." Willie cried out mocking Chaz. Thad and Donny burst into laughter.

"Man shut up and pass that shit." Chaz said. "So country boy, how you like it up here so far?"

"It's different from Alabama. Took a while to get

used to."

"Heard about Dino," Donny asked. "The pigs ain't never gettin' him for that one. I heard he's in Pennsylvania."

"Dumb ass nigga," said Willie. He took a puff then passed it to Thad. "All they had to do was jump 'em then leave 'em alone."

"Yeah but you know Dino." Chaz said. "They found his boy Taylor in a dumpster off 132nd. One of Reg niggas did that."

Thad took a puff and looked at the little bit of skyline he could see from the old rusted fire escape. He wasn't paying much attention to the conversation. He was in his own world. He was tired of hearing all of the bad in Harlem. Thad started to imagine what his friends were going say when he told them all of the things he saw and experienced while in Harlem. He took another puff of the joint and then passed it. Donny took the tin container out of his pocket and handed it to Willie. Willie pulled out a pack of rolling papers and started to roll another joint. He took a few pinches of the green pungent smelling substance and placed it into the paper.

"How'd you learn that," Thad asked.

"Practice," said Willie.

"And he learned it from me," Chaz said.

"I taught you how to roll."

"And in what reality is that?"

"The one we in now nigga." Willie said.

Willie finished rolling the second joint then started to roll a third. He handed one to Thad and the other to Donny. "Last one." Willie said as he started to roll a fourth. "Smoke 'til you choke." Donny said. Thad lit his joint then passed the lighter to Donny. The boys continued to joke around and talk as the smoke from their joints filled the air like a locomotive chugging across the open plains of Kansas. Thad was beginning to feel lightheaded. He felt euphoric. Now he knew what Willie was talking about earlier. It was something he couldn't explain but it felt good.

"Hey what time is it," Donny asked.

"A little past one, why?" Willie said.

"Oh shit, my brother should be downstairs. Chaz you need a ride home?"

"Hell yeah.Police ain't grabbin' me up tonight. I'll

see yall later."

Willie walked Donny and Chaz to the front door and let them out. Thad laid down on the couch while his head spun around the room.

"How you feelin?" Willie asked.

"Tired, hungry, and high as a kite."

Willie and Thad laughed. They both got up and fixed themselves a plate of spaghetti and sat at the kitchen table. Smoking on the fire escape was the most fun Thad had in a long time. If all he did was smoke and listen to the radio for the next two weeks, then Thad's vacation would turn out to be a splendid one in his mind.

"I got one more." Willie said while holding another joint in his hand. "Wanna smoke it?"

"Sure." Thad said. They finished eating then went into Willie's room. "That Window open?" Willie asked. When Thad saw it was still open he nodded his head yes. Willie pulled the chair in the corner over to the window.

"I'm glad you came up." Willie said.

"Me too. You know this ain't as bad as adults say. I don't even see why it's illegal."

"You got me."

"Maybe they'll legalize it one day." Thad suggested.

"Doubt it. Anything niggas do for have fun the law finds a way to throw us in jail for it. Black, White, it don't matter to them. Anything fun, they get rid of it."

"I don't think it works like that." Thad said. "They'll legalize it one day. Then everybody can get high and relax with no worries."

"That'll be a great day."

When they finished up the joint Thad laid down on his stomach as Willie laid down on the floor. "What's it like havin' sisters?"

"It's ok. Ever since my dad died it got a lot tougher around here. Now I gotta be the man of the house and I ain't even grown yet."

"How'd he die?"

"Got killed a few blocks from here. Some dude tried to rob him for a few bucks."

"Just some random guy shot your dad?"

"Naw, some junkie stabbed 'em."

The room went silent. Then the boys heard someone start to play a saxophone outside. Willie and Thad sat and listened. As the person continued to play Willie fell asleep. Thad stayed awake to listen to the music. It was beautiful. It was slowly paced and had a soothing melody. Thad was anxious to see if it was the same guy from the other night. When he sat up to look out the window he saw that it was. The young man still looked dirty and unkept. Thad continued to watch him play until Willie woke up. "That nigga still playin'?" he said. He stood up and walked over to the window. "That horse got him all messed up now. Look at him." Thad looked at the young man. What ever horse was Thad knew it was bad. When he turned around to ask Willie what horse was, he had already left and went out into the living room. Thad continued to watch the man play until he stopped about twenty minutes later. The man reached into his pocket and pulled something out. After looking at whatever it was that he pulled out he put it back into his pocket. The young man started up the street with his saxophone in hand. He looked fatigued, tired, and beat up. Thad watched him walk up the street until he was out of sight. "What a jungle." Thad said. He turned off the light and went to bed.

Chapter 7

The next morning Thad felt great. He was the first one up besides Aunt Bird who was in the kitchen enjoying a cup of coffee. After he took a bath Thad went into the living room to listen to the radio. He was surprised to see Willie who was usually already out of the house by the time the rest of the family got up. When Thad sat down Willie looked up at him, "What you plan on doin' tonight," he said.

"I don't know, what you plannin' to do?"

"I gotta go get somethin' from the store. Donny said his brother got em a car. We might just ride around tonight and drink a bit."

By now Thad felt as though he had experienced the worst of Harlem. Riding around with Willie and his friends couldn't hurt. "Sure. Ain't nothin' else for me to do."

"Cool," Willie said. He ran to the kitchen to tell his mom he and Thad were heading out. Thad slipped on his shoes as Willie grabbed his. They got on the elevator and went to the first floor. When they got outside Thad saw the young man with the saxophone. He was sitting on the front steps of a building. Ever since Willie brought it up Thad had been wondering what "horse" was. The only thing he knew about it was that it was the stuff the guy with the saxophone would stand on the corner and wait for almost every night. Over the past week Thad started to realize the guy's condition was worsening. He looked as if he was losing a fight.

After walking for a few blocks the boys arrived at Wilson's Liquor Store. It was a small corner store at the end of Willie's block. Willie told Thad to wait outside. While Thad sat outside of the store he looked around for a bit soaking up the surrounding scenery. Across the street a woman pushing a stroller was approached by a tall older gentleman who could barely stand up straight. He asked the young woman a question who quickly turned him away. The man looked around until he saw Thad. Thad knew the old man was coming over to ask him the same question. The man stunk of dried urine and alcohol. "Excuse me brotha," the man said, "can you spare me a little change please so I can get somethin' to eat?"

"I don't have nothin' on me sir. Sorry."

"C'mon man, don't lie. I know you sellin' that shit. All I want is a little change."

The old man was becoming belligerent, "Look man, I don't have nothin' on me!" Thad shouted. Willie came out of the store with a brown paper bag in his hand. The man looked up at Willie, "Can you spare some-". Before the man could even finish his sentence Willie cut him off. "Man get the hell outta my face. My cousin ain't got shit and I don't either."

The old drunk gave both of the boys a scowl before walking away. "Who was that," Thad asked. "Probably just some old whino askin for booze money. You alright?"

"Yeah." Now was the perfect time for Thad to ask Willie what horse was. "Hey I got a question," he said, "what's horse?"

"Some wicked shit. It's this brown powder that almost look like flour. A bunch of niggas around here like to use it."

"What is it?"

"Ever heard of a narcotic?" Thad nodded his head yes, "Well that's what it is."

"So it's a drug?"

"Yeah. You heat it up in a spoon then put a syringe to it. After that you just inject it."

"What does it do to you?"

"You get high off of it but the high ain't one I want. I heard the shit can kill you."

"You think that guy with the saxophone use it?"

"I know he do, that stuff is heavy around here. For some reason musicians love it"

"How could someone so talented ever turn to that stuff," he thought. Then Thad remembered Lil' Fitz, the little boy Thad met on the train. He was somewhere roaming the country with his dad who was addicted to this drug. Thad felt sick to his stomach knowing that a kid that young was under the care of a drug addict. Knowing that Lil' Fitz had no way of ever getting back to his mom and that he didn't know what his dad was doing made Thad upset. If he had known at the time he would have said something to one of the rail workers but now it was too late. Lil' Fitz and his dad had gotten off the train back in a Chicago well over a week ago, They could have been across the country by now. "Hey Willie, can I tell you something'?"

"What's up?"

"When I was on the train I met this kid from Baltimore and he said his dad picked him up from school but I know his dad really kidnapped him. He told me his dad uses that stuff. They don't even have a place to stay. They just hop trains and go city to city while his dad runs hustles. Is horse that bad?" Willie took a while to answer. He just looked at Thad with a somber face. There was no way Willie could sugar coat it. "Damn, all I can say is pray for the kid. His life ain't gon be too pretty from here on out." Thad became grief stricken. All he could do was picture Lil' Fitz's smile before he and his dad headed to another car on the train. Willie gave Thad a pat on the back as they headed back to Willie's apartment.

When they got back home Willie slipped into his room with Thad and set the small brown bag in his closet. "That's the party juice," he said. "Donny and Chaz should be here around midnight, I think we stoppin' by a party for a few." What happened at the last party had long since become nothing more than a memory to Thad. He was ready to go out and have a good time with Willie and his friends.

Later that night Aunt Bird left for work like usual at around eight. The girls ate dinner then went into the living room to play with their dolls. Since he and Thad weren't leaving out until later Willie decided to let the girls stay up a little later than usual before sending them to bed at around eleven.

"Man tonight Ima have a good ass time." Willie said. "What you plan on doin' tonight?" Thad though about it long and hard. The only thing he wanted to do was see Ashley again. The thought of her bright smile and the smell of her perfume made his heart melt. "I ain't ask you to solve an equation nigga," Willie said.

"I would love to see that girl Ashley again."

Willie looked at Thad in disbelief. "Out of all the possibilities in the world, this nigga wanna see some broad he only met once. You don't even know her. What you smitten by he looks?"

"I really like her. She's nice and pretty. Just how I like 'em."

Willie sat down and put his arm around Thad. "Thad, I know down south straight hair on a black girl is rare but listen, that shit is normal up here."

Thad gave Willie a playful shove as they both laughed. Thad decided this was the night to put on his suit. His grandmother made him pack one in case Aunt Bird decided to take the family to church. He wanted to look sharp in the event he saw Ashley again and to keep Willie and Chaz off of his back. Willie hopped in the shower while Thad got dressed. Midway through buttoning his shirt Thad looked outside and saw the guy with the saxophone. Two men were standing next to him and engaging in conversation. The young man was literally down on his knees begging these men for a fix. Thad finally saw the full extent of what this drug could do. It had made this man a victim. This talented and skilled musician was now just a starving and powerless junkie. After what looked like pleading the man handed over his shiny brass saxophone to the two men. One of them threw some drugs at him and walked away. Weeping, the young man picked his drugs up off of the pavement. For possibly the last time Thad watched the guy walk off into the night until he was out of sight.

Thad pulled the shade down and sat on the edge of

the bed. He was disturbed by what he had just witnessed. He went back to buttoning his shirt and thought about his and Willie's night. Before they left, Willie and Thad went out back to have a quick smoke. Willie checked his watch and saw it was almost midnight. He finished up the joint then flicked it over the rail. Willie locked up the apartment then slipped back out onto the fire escape. When they got out front Donny was pulling up in a shiny burgundy Packard. The only cars Thad was used to seeing were old rusted pickups with manure or animal feed loaded up in the bed

"What you guys think?" Donny said. "Beauty ain't she?"

"Whoo-ooh! Where'd you get this one from?" Willie asked.

"My brother said some guy wanted it compacted. He said I could drive it around for the night." Thad wondered why would a brand new car like this need to be destroyed. It didn't even look a year old. Thad had a funny feeling about the car but he and Willie got in it anyway. If he had the chance at that moment Thad would have gotten out of the car, went back upstairs, got undressed and went to sleep. By the time he finished his thought the car had already sped off. Chaz pulled out a large bottle of liquor from between his legs that had been sitting on the floor. He had snuck it from his father's cabinet. He took a large swig then passed it around the car. Donny took a big swig then handed it back to Chaz. "Goddamn Chaz, what is that?" Donny asked as he grimaced.

"Just a little dark whiskey. Man up, might put some hair on ya chest." he said. Willie took a swig and passed it to Thad who just looked at it. He took the bottle and handed it back to Chaz who took another swig before putting the top back on the now almost empty bottle. The car was silent for a while until Chaz began to run his mouth like usual. "Watch me score one today." he said. "Willie what you thinking'? I know I got a few lil' broads waitin on a nigga tonight."

"Ima just be humble tonight, let you get some spotlight for once," Willie said.

"Chaz always got the spotlight. The chicks dig me more than the band most the time."

Thad wasn't paying the other boys any attention. They joked around until the car pulled up to an old abandoned building much like the one from Thad's first night in Harlem. They all got out of the car and walked across the street to the back of another building. "What's with all these abandoned buildins' yall go to?" Thad asked.

"They be the best ones," Chaz said. He walked up to the door and knocked. A slit opened up with someone on the other side. "Open up nigga you know it's me," Chaz said. The door opened up with a large man standing in the doorway like the one from the last party. "See, I got us in for free. Imagine what these girls gon' say when they see me." The boys walked in as they immediately heard music. This time Thad knew what the weird smell was that was in the air. It was the smell of alcohol and marijuana.

Thad tugged on Willie's sleeve, "How long we gon' be here?"

"Not too long. Chaz wanted to come here so we just stoppin' by."

Chaz hopped on the first girl he saw. He grabbed her and became engulfed by the sea of intoxicated dancing teenagers. Donny had also disappeared into the crowd leaving Willie in the middle of the floor by himself. When Donny reappeared he had a beer in each hand. "Where'd everybody go?" he said. "Chaz is dancin' with every girl he see and Thad walked off. Donny handed Willie a beer. "Just get a few of these in you," he said. Donny walked over to a chair and sat down while he tapped his foot and snapped his fingers to the music. It was uncharacteristic for him to be up and dancing. Donny liked to sit and drink while listening to music.

On the other side of the room Thad was sitting down and enjoying the music in his own way. The trumpet, saxophone player, and drummer were all in sync tonight. Their music gave the entire room a breath and pulse of it's own. Thad could feel the floorboards under his feet moving and shaking as his peers danced the night away. Then he felt a tap on his shoulder. When he turned around hc couldn't believe it. Standing right there in front of him was Ashley. Her perfect smile, beautiful brown eyes, and long pretty dark brown hair seemed to have taken on an extra glow since their last encounter. Thad was at a loss for words. Her heavenly figure and beautiful fragrance had him entranced.

"So you want me to say hi first?" she asked?

"Hey Ashley," he said. His voice cracked a little under the pressure. Last time he had the courage of a few beers in his system. This time he was going off of pure confidence, or in this instance his lack of it.

"What you doin' here?" he asked.

"A few of my friends dragged me here. I just wanted to stay home but they insisted."

"Yeah me too. You wanna dance for a few songs?"

Ashley smiled, "I would like that." Thad took her hand and the two started towards the dance floor.

Across the room Chaz had become the life of the party. He was bouncing around the room and switching dance partners more than the band switched notes. The ones he found to be the prettiest got a long smooch before being left for the next girl. By now Donny was sloppy drunk but he continued to pound back every beer that touched his hands. Willie was the only one not a having a great time. He had noticed how drunk Donny had gotten but Donny was the only one who knew how to drive. Willie grabbed Chaz when the band finished their number and told him they had to leave.

"We ain't even been here a hour and he passed out," Chaz said. He looked over and saw Donny was slumped over. "Alright man, find ya cousin and lets get outta here." While Willie looked for Thad, he and Ashley had sat down at a table to talk.

"This has got to be the hottest it's been since I got here." he said. "Almost feel like home."

"Does it ever snow in Alabama?"

"Rarely, and if it does it ain't that much."

"You got a girlfriend back home?

"No. Why you ask?"

"Just wonderin'. What are the girls like down there anyway?"

"Like you but not as pretty. If you came to Alabama you'd be the prettiest girl in the entire State." Ashley blushed.

Willie was still frantically searching for Thad who seemed to disappear. No one had seen him and looking for him in the crowded room was difficult. Donny was inebriated and Chaz was giving a half assed search because he was still caught up in the girls. The band leader stepped up to the mic to make an announcement.

"Alright cool cats and swingettes, this is our last number then it's time to split. A one, two, a one, two, three, four…" Right when the music started there was a small part in the crowd. Willie could see Thad sitting at a table with Ashley. He didn't want to interrupt but he had to tell Thad it was time to leave. He walked over and grabbed Thad, "Hey we gotta split, Donny is drunk as hell and he's the only one who can drive." Thad didn't want to leave Ashley but he had to. Thad's first kiss was one he could be proud of, he grabbed Ashley and stood up . Before she could say anything he kissed her. "Hope I can see you again." he said before Willie led him away.

When they got back to the table Donny was passed out laying on top of the table. Willie grabbed Chaz and told him to help carry Donny down stairs. "Check his pockets for the keys," Thad said. Chaz went into Donny's pocket and pulled out the car key. He opened the door and pushed Donny inside. Willie hopped in the passenger's side while Chaz got into the driver's seat. "How do I start it?"

"Press on the brake and turn the key," Thad said. Willie and Chaz looked at Thad

"You now how to drive?" Willie said.

"Not really. I drove a tractor." Chaz pressed down on the brake and turned the key as the car started. "This the plan, Ima get us a few blocks from here," Chaz said, "then we ditchin' the car. Donny said it was gettin' scrapped in the mornin' anyway. I'll take him to my house to sleep this off. Got it?" Willie and Thad agreed before Chaz pressed on the gas and took off. As the car whizzed down the street Willie and Thad held on for their lives. The boys made it maybe five blocks before almost slamming into another car. "Slow down!" Willie yelled. Chaz slammed on the brakes as everyone braced themselves to keep from flying out of the front winshield. Donny hit the back of Willie's seat before slamming back into his seat.

"Damn nigga. What was that?" Willie said.

"Then you drive." Chaz said.

"We close to yo house anyway. Lets just get out." Chaz grabbed Donny and the car keys. Willie and Thad ran to the side of a building to stay out of sight of any passing cops.

"I'll walk him to my house and call his brother." Chaz said "Yall alright?"

"Yeah." Willie said. "We gon cross that empty field and cut through that old buildin behind my street. Yall be safe man." Thad and Willie split up from Chaz and an inebriated Donny. "Alright. This what we gon do," Willie started, "When traffic slows way down we'll jet across the street. There's an empty field a few blocks away. When we get across the field that old building behind my house is right there." Due to the heavy influx of violence in the neighborhood that summer, the district decided to step up their patrols. As long as they stayed out of sight Thad and Willie would be home free.

"How far until the field?" Thad asked.

"About three or four blocks."

"We don't have to run do we?"

"Not if we stay hidden from the cops."

Thad didn't want to run in his dress shoes. They weren't the most comfortable shoes to walk in so running in them would be even worse. After walking for a few blocks Thad and Willie made it to the street with the empty field. They walked up to the gate and looked it all the way up. Thad climbed over first. When he got over the top he ran across the field and hid behind some bushes.

Willie checked around to make sure no one was looking. Right before he reached the top Willie's jacket got caught in the gate. When he finally wiggled it loose he felt a firm hand grab his leg. The hand yanked him down off of the gate and onto the ground. When Willie looked up two police officers were standing directly over him.

As Thad watched everything unfold Willie hoped the officers didn't see Thad who was still behind the bushes nervously watching. As the cops threw Willie into the back of the car one of the cops grabbed his flashlight and shined it in Thad's direction. He ducked down as low as he could and prayed the cop didn't see him. "Your buddy's stayin' in the precinct tonight." the cop said. "All for you." He turned around and got into the car. When the car pulled off Thad remained hidden for several minutes. He didn't know what else to do. He was sacred, alone, and most of all lost. He would be damned if he was going to walk through that old abandoned building alone. Thad got up brushed off his pants and jacket and started walking towards the end of the field. He was going to take his chances and walk the busy strip home. It was the easiest way to get back home and the only way he knew.

Chapter 8

As Thad continued down the main street the constant sound of cars driving past made him nervous. With each passing vehicle he stood the chance of a patrolman stopping Thad and taking him in. Thad had never been this scared in his life. He couldn't help but to think the worst. "They probably beat him up on the way to the station," he thought. That sort of thing was normal down south. Thad had heard too many horror stories of town sheriffs arresting people only to never be seen or heard from again. He slipped down an alley way and sat there for a minute leaning his back against a wall. He reached into his pocket and felt crumbs wrapped up in a piece of paper. When he pulled it out it was a joint that Willie gave him to save for the ride back home. By now it had fallen apart. He stuffed it back into his pocket wishing he had a lighter on hand. This was the type of stress that warranted a quick smoke.

In the distance Thad could hear some music playing. He listened to the tune for a moment as he calmed himself down. He knew Willie was headed to jail and there was nothing he could do about it. Thad decided to focus all of his energy into getting home. Down the street from where Thad sat to collect himself was a nightclub that was still open. There wasn't much else happening on the street so it wasn't hard to hear the music a block away. When he finally made his way to the building there were two big doors that sat wide open revealing another set of smaller doors that were closed. Thad walked through the smaller doors and looked around for someone who could give him directions back to Willie's apartment building. He didn't know the street or address but he did know the name of the building. When he looked around there was a man sitting at a piano talking to a man with a saxophone around his neck as the two of them shared a drink. At the bar was a bartender who looked around Thad's grandmother's age. He was wiping down the bar when he saw Thad standing in the middle of the floor. "Hey kid," he said. "Come on in." Thad walked in and sat at the bar directly in front of the bartender.

"Damn boy, you look beat the hell up," he said. "Rough night?"

"Very rough." Thad said.

"Want a soda? It's on the house."

"Please, thank you."

"Where you from kid? You sound like you from down south."

"Beloit, Alabama. Came up here to visit family."

"I know Beloit. I'm from Mississippi. Came up here when I was only 16. Say what's your name anyway kid?"

"Thad." The bartender smiled and walked away. He tapped the piano player on the shoulder and whispered something in his ear. The bartender took some money out of his pocket and handed it to the piano player. He walked back over to the bar and poured himself a drink. After the type of night he just had Thad needed an ice cold soda and some music to unwind.

"My name's Oliver by the way."

"Nice to meet you," Thad said.

"I gotta close up in a few but you can stay until the song's over."

"Don't worry, I'll be gone. Can you tell me where the Langston Homes are?"

"Sure. You go straight down this street then take a right at the stop light. You should see a liquor store on the corner called-"

"Wilson's?" Thad interrupted.

"Yeah. Langston homes should be right down the street.

"Thanks again sir."

"No problem Thad."

Thad finished up his soda and listened to the band mates until they finished up their number. The piano player continued to play as his band mate packed up his saxophone. With clear directions Thad grabbed his jacket and swung it over his back. He walked out of the Jazz club and started down the street. Outside he could hear the sounds of another Harlem summer night. Distant sirens and cars periodically passing by gave him a city soundtrack to walk home to. When he finally made it back to Willie's building Thad went up the fire escape and walked over to the window. Willie usually left it unlocked in the case he ever lost his key. Thad slipped in through the window then went to go check on the girls who were still asleep. Thad walked into Willie's room and got undressed. He laid down and went to sleep almost immediately.

As Thad slept he began to have a dream where he was walking down a long, dark, and narrow hallway. As he continued down the dark and mysterious corridor there was a burst of light coming from behind him. He turned around and saw two lights shining brightly in his direction. As he stood looking at the lights they began to grow larger and larger as if they were coming towards him. It took Thad a second to realize the lights were the headlights of a car. As he began to run down the hall the headlights seemed to be gaining on him. He looked down and noticed he was running in place. Further down the hall there was a door on the left. Thad ran as fast as he could but he still hadn't made any progress. When he looked back the car showed no signs of slowing down. There was a bright flash of light as Thad braced for the impact. When he opened his eyes there were two cops were standing over his bloody and beaten body. They both pulled out their guns and pointed them at his face. Before they fired their first shots Thad woke up.

He heard a knock at the door that startled him. He assumed it was one of the girls since no one else was there. He got out of bed and opened the door to see Daisy.

"Where's Willie?" she asked. "I checked on the couch but he not there." Thad knew he couldn't tell Daisy the truth, especially about something this serious.

"Maybe he sleepin' at some girl's house or something'," he said.

"He helps me sleep when I have bad dreams."

"You had a bad dream too?" Daisy nodded yes. "I'll tell you what," Thad said "lets go sleep on the couch until our nightmares go away."

"Ok." she said. Thad and Daisy went into the living room to sleep on the couch. He sat up as she rested her head on his lap. "I don't like when Willie stays out late." she said.

"What you mean?"

Daisy rolled over and looked at Thad, "When he hangs out with his friends. Mommy told me one night when my daddy left out real late and he never came back because somebody killed him. I don't want Willie to get stabbed."

All Thad could do was look out he window as his little cousin's head rested on his lap. "Trust me, he'll be ok," he said. Thad wasn't sure if Willie was ok or not. All he knew was that Willie was in a jail cell somewhere. Daisy yawned and drifted off to sleep. Thad leaned his head back and closed his eyes.

When Thad woke up the next morning the apartment was eerily quiet. He noticed Daisy wasn't laying on him anymore so he got up and grabbed his toothbrush before heading into the bathroom. He walked over to Aunt Bird's bedroom door and pressed his ear up against it. Since he didn't hear anything Thad decided to open the door and peek in. Both Daisy and Denise were fast asleep but Aunt Bird hadn't come in yet. Aunt Bird was usually home by eight o'clock and it was a quarter past nine. He figured she would be home at any moment wondering where her son was.

After Thad got dressed he poured himself a glass of orange juice and went into the living room to listen to the radio. He had to think of something he could tell the girls when they got up and saw Willie wasn't home. The hardest part would be trying to cover for Willie to Aunt Bird. Thad had no idea what he was going to say or do. When Denise walked in she let out a big yawn. "Where my brother at?" she said. Thad blankly stared at her.

"Hey. Alabama," she said "where…is…my…bother? Understand?"

"I don't know." he said. "Maybe he left out or somethin'."

"Who gon' cook me somethin' to eat then?"

Thad was relieved he didn't have to answer anymore questions about Willie's whereabouts. "I can make you some oatmeal on the stove." he said.

Denise turned her face up in disappointment. "I'll take it." she said. Denise walked into the kitchen with Thad following behind her. She reached into the cabinet over the stove and pulled out a large oatmeal container. She walked over to another cabinet and grabbed a cooking pot. She set it on the stove then looked at Thad. "I like mines made with milk," she said. She looked over towards the refrigerator as if she was pointing with her eyes. Thad looked back at her for a moment before walking over to the sink with the pot to fill it up with water. "I said milk!"

"And I'm usin' water. You could just not eat," Thad snapped. Denise put on a pout and took a seat at the table. Thad turned on the stove and made the oatmeal. He knew it wouldn't be long before Daisy got out of bed so he decided to make enough for the three of them. Thad made himself and Denise each a bowl and sat down. Denise ate a spoonful of her oatmeal, "A little lumpy but it's ok," she said. "I bet Willie got arrested again."

Thad choked on his oatmeal, "Arrested?" he said. "What makes you say that?"

"Because, every time he not here in the mornin' he be in jail."

"For what

"My momma never tell me and Daisy. They probably in a cab right now. She callin' him a dumbass and Willie just sittin' there lookin stupid." Denise shook her head as if she was disgusted. Not long after, Daisy walked in while rubbing her eyes.

"Where's Willie" she asked.

"In jail" Denise answered.

"Again?"

"Nobody's in jail," Thad said. "I made oatmeal, you want some?"

Daisy nodded her head yes as she took a seat at the table. Thad fixed her a bowl and sat it down in front of her. Daisy took a spoonful and blew on it. "Lumpy but it's ok," she said. After breakfast the girls got washed up and went to their friend Alisha's to go play. Thad went into the living room to listen to the radio. He could hear some indistinct chatter coming from the hallway. He leaned over as he turned the radio down to get a better listen. He made out Aunt Bird's voice and an older gentleman. The door opened up and Willie walked in. He was all in one piece with no bruises or marks. He walked in and looked at Thad with a smirk on his face as he walked to his room. Thad looked up at the door and saw the officer that had arrested Willie the night before. Thad was hoping the officer didn't recognize him. He felt his stomach drop and his skin get warm and tingly with nervousness. The cop turned his head and continued his conversation with Aunt Bird.

"Like I said, just be happy our precinct got him ma'am and not another one," he said.

"Thank you so much," Aunt Bird said. The officer gave her a tip of his cap before walking down the hall. Aunt Bird walked in and closed the door. She sat down on the couch and let out a long sigh. "Good morning Thad.

Where are the girls?"

Thad was still surprised the officer didn't recognize him, although he was hiding behind some bushes. "At Alisha's." he said.

"Good. Me and Willie need to talk." She got up and went into Willie's room. Thad didn't know what Aunt Bird and Willie were talking about. All he knew was that he was in the clear. After having that close of a call Thad decided to spend his remaining two weeks in Harlem confined to the small two bedroom apartment.

When Willie and Aunt Bird finally came out of Willie's room, Willie's entire demeanor had changed. His head was low as his shoulders drooped. He went into the bathroom to take a bath as Aunt Bird went into her room. Thad wondered what Aunt Bird said to Willie that caused his mood to change so quickly and drastically. He figured it to be the usual disciplinary scolding. After Willie was done with his shower he went out into the living room and sat down on the couch. There was an unsettling silence that fell upon the two boys for a moment. "My mom sendin' you home early," he said.

Thad's heart sank into his stomach. He wasn't ready

to leave just yet. "Why?"

"She said I ain't responsible enough or some shit to have company. Said I put you and the girls in danger. Can't leave the house for a month."

"When am I leavin'?"

"Tomorrow. She wanted me to tell you myself."

"Am I in any trouble?"

"Naw. Yo name never came up."

The both of them just sat there. Willie had rescued Thad for the last time. Thad tried to be optimistic about the situation. "Don't get too down," he said, "We got all day today to hang out."

"Doin' what? I'm stuck in here for a month."

When Aunt Bird walked in she sat down and offered Thad an apology. "Sorry we have to send you home so early sweetheart," she said. "I already called Grandma and explained the situation."

"It's ok," Thad said. "I did enjoy myself. Hopefully I can come back again and visit."

"That would be nice," she said. Aunt Bird smiled then went back into her room.

Later that night Aunt Bird got ready for work as

usual. After having to go and pick up Willie from jail she decided to try and get her shift changed. "Tonight may be my last third shift so you better enjoy it," she said. She turned to Thad and changed her tone to a less authoritative one, "We're leaving as soon as I get home, your train is leaving at about 8:30 so be ready." She grabbed her purse and went into her room. When the girls got back and saw Willie they were all giggles. To them whenever Willie got into this much trouble they found it amusing.

Later that evening after dinner the girls went into the living room to listen to their favorite program while Willie and Thad went into Willie's room.

"I still got some grass to smoke if you want to." Willie said.

"I still got one too but it's a little mashed up."

"When they go to sleep we'll step out."

After the girls' program went off Willie got them ready for bed. Once they were in bed Willie waved for Thad to come with him into the kitchen. Thad got up and followed Willie onto the fire escape. The two boys sat down and leaned up against the building. Willie pulled a joint from behind his ear and lit it. "Last night was wild wasn't it?" he said.

"Yeah it was. I thought the cops was comin' for me next."

"If they would've grabbed you too my mom would've left me in there and bailed you out. She think I need to be left in jail anyway." Willie took a strong puff then passed it to Thad.

"Thanks for not rattin' me out."

"C'mon man. I can't ever see myself stoopin' that low. That's a rule you never break in the streets."

Thad took another puff of the joint then passed it to Willie. "I miss that guy playin' his saxophone. I'm gonna miss this period." he said.

"Miss what?"

"Smokin' on this fire escape listenin' to this city that never really sleeps. Can't wait to come back when I'm older."

"You really wanna come back and visit?"

"Yeah, I wanna see more of the city next time. And the girls are like little sisters. Especially Daisy."

"Good. Take 'em with you, especially Denise.

"Nah, you can keep her."

As the two laughed they finished up their last joint together. Thad took in the bright city sky and sounds of the metropolitan backdrop. When they were done smoking Thad and Willie went back inside. Willie went into the living room to lay down. Thad thought it would be more convenient if he packed before he went to sleep. When he was finished packing, Thad looked out the window and at the corner. There was no saxophone, no gun shots, no nothing. Just the city.

The next morning was a somber one. Thad got out of bed and went to his suitcase. He pulled out a shirt and a pair of slacks then closed it. When he got up to go into the bathroom Willie and Denise were in the kitchen. Thad brushed his teeth and went to his favorite spot for the past week. The phone rang as Willie came into the living room to answer it. When he hung up Willie told Thad Aunt Bird was on her way. When Thad went to go grab his bags he took one last look around the room.

When he walked out of the room he was met by the girls. "Bye Thad." they said in unison as they each gave him a big hug.

"See ya," he said. Willie took one of Thad's bags and the two walked to the elevator. Neither one of them could said a word. When they got outside Aunt Bird's taxi hadn't pulled up yet. They decided to sit down on the curb and wait for her.

"How long it take you to get back home?" Willie asked.

"I don't know, I'm taking a different train this time."

"Oh. Well be safe."

Right then a bright yellow taxi pulled up. Willie and Thad knew it was Aunt Bird. They both stood up and grabbed a bag. After they put the bags in the trunk of the cab Willie gave Thad a strong dap. "See ya man. Take care of yourself" he said.

"You too," Thad said before getting into the taxi. As the driver pulled off Thad watched the crumbled cityscape he was beginning love pass him by. He didn't know the next time he was going to see Harlem or if he ever would again for that matter.

"Sorry your time got cut short," Aunt Bird said. "Hope you enjoyed yourself."

"I did. Me and Willie have to keep in touch."

"He might be going away soon," she said "but I'll make sure you guys do."

Thad wasn't sure what that meant but he knew it wasn't good. He wanted to ask but knew it meant most likely meant Willie was in more trouble than he thought. Thad just kept his mouth shut and enjoyed the ride. When the cab pulled up to the station Aunt Bird got out to help Thad unload his bags. "Want me to wait with you or are you alright?" she asked.

"I'm ok."

"Well you be safe and it was a pleasure." She gave Thad a big hug and kiss on the cheek before getting back into the cab. Thad watched the cab drive off until it was out of his sight. His time in Harlem had officially come to an end. He went to one of the ticket windows and got himself a ticket. This time he would be on a train headed straight for Alabama with no stops. Thad walked out to the platform and waited for his train to come. He still had a lot of money leftover from the money his grandmother had given him before he left. He bought himself a few sodas for the ride then sat down on an empty bench. He opened one of the sodas and began to drink it.

He opened up one of his bags to put the other soda in it when he felt a bulge in the bottom of his suit case. It was a metal tin that had a few buds of marijuana in it with a note. Thad took the note out and looked at it before shoving it into his pocket. He put the tin back into his bag and closed it. A few moments later Thad could hear a large silver train barreling down the tracks. He grabbed his ticket and waited to board. "Next stop," he thought to himself " sweet home Beloit, Alabama." Thad boarded and prepared himself for the long and boring train ride. As the train began to pull out of the station, Thad watched the buildings and the New York skyline gradually disappear. He pulled Willie's note out of his pocket and began to read it.

About the Author

Brendan Whitt is an author and freelance journalist based in Cleveland, Ohio. He first discovered his love for writing at the age of 13. Brendan holds a B.A. in Journalism from Cleveland State University. Brendan's writing can be found on his blog "When Brendan Whitt Thinks…". His writing has also been featured in the *Call & Post Cleveland* newspaper and Cleveland blog *Volume Magazine Cleveland*.

Brendan Whitt has also published two poetry collections, also available online now through Amazon and Kindle. To keep up with Brendan follow him on both Twitter (@BrendanWhitt) and Instagram (@SneakersMcGee) and like his Facebook page (Brendan the Writer).

www.ingramcontent.com/pod-product-compliance
Lightning Source LLC
Chambersburg PA
CBHW052146170626
46812CB00004B/1606